Powerful, prominent, proud—the Oklahoma Wentworths' greatest fortune was family. So when they discovered that pregnant mom-to-be Sabrina Jensen was carrying the newest Wentworth heir—and had vanished without a trace—they vowed to...Follow That Baby!

Follow That Baby

Josie Wentworth: The socialite knew luxury living—not working ranches and recalcitrant ranchers! But a love letter to Sabrina Jensen and a diamond ring had brought her to the Single C and...

Max Carter: One minute, the granite-chiseled cowboy was giving the heave-ho to the pampered princess. The next, he was nursing the amnesiac beauty to health—and trying hard not to fall in love....

Joseph Wentworth: The stalwart patriarch of Wentworth Oil Works had raised his three grandchildren from rug rats to respectable adults. Now his oldest grandson was gone...and Josie had run off half-cocked to find some answers....

Sabrina Jensen: Max's pregnant cousin's whereabouts were a mystery—until a baby doctor's bill provided the first clue....

* * * *

Don't miss THE DADDY AND THE BABY DOCTOR by Kristin Morgan, next month's Follow That Baby title, available in Silhouette Romance.

Dear Reader,

Autumn inspires visions of the great outdoors, but Special Edition lures you back inside with six vibrant romances!

Many of the top-selling mainstream authors today launched their careers writing series romance. Some special authors have achieved remarkable success in the mainstream with both hardcovers and paperbacks, yet continue to support the genre and the readers they love. *New York Times* bestselling author Nora Roberts is just such an author, and this month we're delighted to bring you *The Winning Hand,* the eighth book in her popular series THE MACGREGORS.

In *Father-to-Be* by Laurie Paige, October's tender THAT'S MY BABY! title, an impulsive night of passion changes a rugged rancher's life forever. And if you enjoy sweeping medical dramas, we prescribe *From House Calls to Husband* by Christine Flynn, part of PRESCRIPTION: MARRIAGE. This riveting new series by three Silhouette authors highlights nurses who vow never to marry a doctor. Look for the second installment of the series next month.

Silhouette's new five-book cross-line continuity series, FOLLOW THAT BABY, introduces the Wentworth oil tycoon family and their search for a missing heir. The series begins in Special Edition this month with *The Rancher and the Amnesiac Bride* by Joan Elliott Pickart, then crosses into Romance (11/98), Desire (12/98), Yours Truly (1/99) and concludes in Intimate Moments (2/99).

Also, check out *Partners in Marriage* by Allison Hayes, in which a vulnerable schoolteacher invades a Lakota man's house—and his heart! Finally, October's WOMAN TO WATCH is talented newcomer Jean Brashear, who unfolds a provocative tale of revenge—and romance—in *The Bodyguard's Bride.*

I hope you enjoy all of the stories this month!

Sincerely,

Karen Taylor Richman
Senior Editor

Joan Elliott Pickart

THE RANCHER AND THE AMNESIAC BRIDE

Published by Silhouette Books
America's Publisher of Contemporary Romance

For Cricket
You were my furry friend for thirteen years.
I miss you, happy girl.

SILHOUETTE BOOKS

Special thanks and acknowledgment are given to Joan Elliott Pickart for her contribution to the Follow That Baby series.

ISBN 0-373-24204-2

THE RANCHER AND THE AMNESIAC BRIDE

This edition published by arrangement with Harlequin Books S.A.

Printed in U.S.A.

Books by Joan Elliott Pickart

Silhouette Special Edition

**Friends, Lovers...and Babies!* #1011
**The Father of her Child* #1025
†*Texas Dawn* #1100
†*Texas Baby* #1141
‡*Wife Most Wanted* #1160
The Rancher and the Amnesiac Bride #1204

Silhouette Desire

**Angels and Elves* #961
Apache Dream Bride #999
†*Texas Moon* #1051
†*Texas Glory* #1088

*The Baby Bet
†Family Men
‡Montana Mavericks: Return to Whitehorn

Previously published under the pseudonym Robin Elliott

Silhouette Special Edition

Rancher's Heaven #909
Mother at Heart #968

Silhouette Intimate Moments

Gauntlet Run #206

Silhouette Desire

Call It Love #213
To Have It All #237
Picture of Love #261
Pennies in the Fountain #275
Dawn's Gift #303
Brooke's Chance #323
Betting Man #344
Silver Sands #362
Lost and Found #384
Out of the Cold #440
Sophie's Attic #725
Not Just Another Perfect Wife #818
Haven's Call #859

JOAN ELLIOTT PICKART

is the author of over seventy novels. When she isn't writing, she enjoys watching football, knitting, reading, gardening and attending craft shows on the town square. Joan has three all-grown-up daughters and a fantastic little grandson. In September of 1995 Joan traveled to China to adopt her fourth daughter, Autumn. Joan and Autumn have settled in to their cozy cottage in a charming, small town in the high pine country of Arizona.

Dear Reader,

Being invited by the Silhouette editors to take part in a special project is a thrill for any author. The FOLLOW THAT BABY series is especially exciting, as the series is traveling through five different Silhouette lines.

Because I wrote the first book in this adventure, I am looking foward to reading the others to see how the continuing story unfolds. Along with you, I will be anticipating the other books like presents to be unwrapped.

While writing *The Rancher and the Amnesiac Bride,* I came to realize how frightening it would be to have amnesia, to look in the mirror and not recognize the person looking back. That is what Josie Wentworth goes through, as she and Max Cooper begin their rocky road to true love.

Josie and Max are from two totally different worlds, which prove very difficult for them to mesh. There are ups and downs, laughter and tears, before they reach their goal of being together, forever.

I sincerely hope you enjoy this first book in the FOLLOW THAT BABY series and the ones that are yet to come.

Thank you all for your support and the lovely letters you write to me. I appreciate all of you more than I can begin to say.

Warmest regards,

Joan Elliott Pickart

Chapter One

The delightful dream Josie Wentworth was having followed her into the foggy state between sleep and wakefulness.

The vivid images in her mind were of her senior prom at Freemont Springs High School. She was wearing a pretty, frilly pink dress, a wrist corsage of gardenias, and her hair was swept up in an extremely sophisticated style.

She was dancing with a lanky, good-looking young man whose name the dream did not supply. A band played louder than necessary in a crepe-paper-decorated gymnasium. She was having an absolutely wonderful time.

Josie stirred, opened her eyes and glanced around the bedroom, fully expecting to see the prom dress in a heap on the floor, where she'd dropped it after the previous night's festivities.

This was the bedroom where she'd grown up, she thought, then yawned. There was her desk, the overflowing bookcase, the dresser—with three drawers spilling forth various items of clothing—the posters on the wall, stuffed animals on a shelf.

But where was the expensive dress with shoes dyed to match? Why couldn't she smell the aroma of gardenias from the now-wilting corsage?

Josie frowned. In the next instant she sat bolt upright in bed, her heart racing. A chill coursed through her as the last vestiges of sleep were shoved away by harsh reality.

She was *not* seventeen years old, she thought, pressing trembling fingertips to her lips. She was *not* a carefree child with license to reminisce at dawn's light about the special dance she'd attended the night before.

She was a twenty-nine-year-old woman who had returned temporarily to her family home to sleep once again in a room where her biggest worry had been if the boy of the moment would telephone as promised.

She was Josie Wentworth, of the notoriously wealthy Oklahoma Wentworth Oil Works family.

She was the granddaughter of Joseph.

The older sister of Michael.

The younger sister of Jack.

And Jack was dead.

A sob caught in Josie's throat and she willed herself not to cry, not again. So many tears she'd shed.

Such pain had ripped through her as she faced, time and again, the horrible truth that she would never see her beloved brother again.

"Oh, God, Jack," she whispered, as the unwelcome tears filled her eyes. "What am I going to do without you? Why did you leave me?" She drew a shaky breath. "Jack—" tears spilled onto her pale cheeks "—be nimble. Jack be quick. Jack jump over..."

Josie shook her head and covered her face with her hands as the raw tears closed her throat.

Two weeks, she thought. It had been two weeks since Trey McGill had telephoned her, asking her to meet him at the Wentworth family estate, where Grandfather and Michael still resided.

Two weeks since a visibly shaken Trey had stood in the enormous living room and taken on the persona of the messenger of death.

He had been with Jack on an undercover mission for the State Department, Trey said. It had been carefully planned down to the most minute detail. Everything was in place. Nothing could go wrong.

But it had all fallen apart, Trey had related, his voice breaking. And Jack...Jack had been killed. His body never recovered. He was gone. Jack Wentworth was gone.

The days since had been a haze of misery for Josie. There'd been so many people to call with the shocking news. A memorial service had been held and she'd told herself over and over that the ceremony *must* give her emotional closure, despite there being no body to lay to eternal rest in the ground.

She was trying so hard to cope, to accept the loss of her big, strong, handsome brother. He had been her hero, always there for her, ready to comfort, protect or praise.

Josie dashed the tears from her cheeks and stared into space, a soft smile forming on her lips as gentle memories momentarily soothed her aching heart.

On her first day of school, she mused, she'd suddenly decided she wasn't going to that scary building she'd visited with her granddad.

The teacher lady smiled all the time and had big teeth and fuzzy hair like a witch. The brightly decorated room she'd seen had been filled with noisy kids, and she didn't like them at all, none of them.

She'd stood in the foyer of the house in her new saddle shoes and knee socks, hating the regulation uniform that was making her itch, and stuck her thumb in her mouth. She refused to budge.

"Let's go, Princess," Joseph Wentworth said. "I promised to drive you to school on the first day and walk you all the way to your classroom, remember? That's exactly what I intend to do, so off we go."

Josie shook her head, then two big tears splashed onto her cheeks.

"There, there, don't cry," Joseph said. "You're a big girl now. My stars, you're five years old and so grown-up. This is a very special and important day for you. Don't you want to show the other children your new shoes?"

Josie sniffled, frowned, then shook her head, her thumb still firmly in her mouth.

"Wonderful," Joseph said, throwing up his hands.

"What should I do? Carry her kicking and screaming into the school building?"

Eleven-year-old Jack set his books on the floor and kneeled in front of Josie.

"Hey, Peanut," Jack said, "listen to me, okay? You and I are going to have a secret code. If you take your thumb out of your mouth, I'll tell you what it is."

Josie studied her big brother for a long moment, then out popped her thumb.

"All right," Jack said, drying Josie's tears with his fingertips. "Here's the deal. When you get scared or upset or lonely, at school or anywhere else, you just say the poem that was written about me and I'll hear you, no matter where I am. You won't see me, but I'll be with you. That's what our secret code will do. Do you remember the poem?"

Josie nodded. "Jack be nimble. Jack be quick. Jack—"

"That's the one," he interrupted. "Do you understand how the secret code works?"

"You'll be with me no matter what," Josie said, nodding. "Even if I can't see you."

"Yep."

"Jack?" Josie said, her bottom lip trembling. "Will the secret code work forever and ever?"

"Forever and ever," he said. "I promise."

"'Kay. I'm ready to go to school now, Granddad."

Joseph Wentworth chuckled. "Jack, you're destined to be a politician when you grow up."

"No," Jack said, getting to his feet. "I'm going

to be a Navy SEABEE. I'll be the best one the navy has ever had."

"I don't doubt that for a minute," Joseph said. "But after you're a famous SEABEE, I'll be waiting for you to take over the running of Wentworth Oil Works. Now hurry along, you two. We don't want to be late."

"Jack be nimble," Josie had whispered as they left the huge house. "Jack be quick...."

Josie shook her head slightly to erase from her mind the scene that had taken place so many years before.

"Forever and ever, Jack?" she said, her own words feeling like physical blows in the quiet room. "Oh, God, Jack, forever is gone."

Downstairs, Joseph Wentworth sipped hot, strong coffee from a wafer-thin china cup. He was in his usual chair at the table in the sun-filled breakfast nook beyond the kitchen, attempting to concentrate on the morning edition of the *Freemont Springs Daily Post.*

With a sigh of defeat he set the paper to one side. Propping his elbows on the table, he cradled the cup in both hands and stared out the window, not actually seeing the perfectly manicured grounds that stretched in all directions.

His oldest grandson was dead, he thought. Jack Wentworth was dead. Maybe if he repeated that horrifying fact often enough, he'd really believe it in his heart, mind and soul.

Maybe he'd be able to let go of the thread of hope

he was clinging to that it was a mistake, that Jack was alive and would walk through the front door any minute. There hadn't been a body to bury, no tangible evidence that—

"Fool," Joseph said aloud. "He's dead and gone, just like his father and mother before him."

This was not the natural order of things. A man shouldn't lose his only son, then years later his oldest grandson. It was too much to bear, too much pain, too stark and cruel.

Joseph set the cup on the saucer, then dragged his hands down his face.

Lord, he was tired. He hadn't slept well since Trey McGill had delivered the unbelievable message of Jack's death.

He sighed.

He was exhausted to the bone, felt every bit of his seventy-two years and then some. He had to get a grip on himself because, heaven knew, he didn't want to have another stroke.

The sound of Josie greeting Evelyn, the housekeeper, reached Joseph and he straightened in his chair. He smoothed his thick, salt-and-pepper hair, then ran one hand over his silk tie. Pulling the newspaper back in front of him, he focused on an article about air pollution.

"Good morning, Granddad," Josie called as she entered the kitchen. "I'll get some coffee and join you if that's all right."

"Hmm?" Joseph dragged his gaze from the paper. "Oh, yes, certainly. You should have more than coffee for breakfast, though."

"That's what Evvie just scolded me about, but I'm really not hungry. Anyway, I'm a bit worried about her. She doesn't look well."

"She's upset about Jack," Joseph said. "After all, she helped me raise him—raise all of you, for that matter. I couldn't have done it without Evelyn's help.

"You and Michael don't remember your parents and the boating accident that killed them, but Evelyn was a pillar of strength during those difficult days. I was very grateful when she agreed to stay on and be a mother figure for you three. She came to love all of you very, very much, believe me."

Josie walked into the sunny nook with a cup of steaming coffee and sat opposite her grandfather. As she sipped the hot drink, Joseph peered at her over the top of the newspaper.

Josie was a beautiful young woman, he thought. She'd inherited the Wentworth dark brown eyes from her father. Her dark auburn hair was a gift from her mother, and Josie wore it in a blunt cut that no doubt had a fancy name. It swung shiny and loose just above her shoulders.

And Josie, his precious little princess, had been crying—again.

"We all love Evvie," Josie said. "She was a wonderful mother to us. I wish I could think of something to say to her to ease her pain, but I can't even do that for myself." She put down her cup. "I hate this, Granddad. I hate it that Jack is... It's not right. It's not fair." She waved one hand in an impatient gesture. "Yes, yes, I know. Whoever said that life was fair?" She sighed and shook her head.

"Drink your coffee," Joseph said gruffly. He snapped the paper back into place and reread the opening paragraph about pollution.

Several minutes passed in total silence.

"Granddad?" Josie said finally.

"Hmm?" He stared unseeing at the newsprint.

"I'm going back to my own apartment today. I can't hide out here any longer, pretending I'm a child within these protective walls. It's time for me to go."

No! Joseph thought with a chilling rush of panic. He didn't want to be alone in this enormous, empty house. He didn't want to be alone with the agonizing pain caused by Jack's death. He didn't want to be alone with his tears that flowed in the dark hours of the night. Dear Lord, Josie, please, no.

"That's fine," he said nonchalantly, lowering the newspaper to look at his granddaughter. "Evelyn and I will get back to our usual routines."

"Yes." Josie paused. "In the last letter I had from Jack, he said that since I was only one year away from being eligible to receive the money from the trust fund you set up for me, I should be giving thought to the possibilities of a career of some sort."

Joseph nodded. "Excellent idea. The terms for the releasing of funds are the same for all three of you. You get the money on your thirtieth birthday or when you marry, whichever comes first. So, find yourself a husband and give your old granddad some great-grandchildren."

"I knew you'd say that," Josie said, laughing. She sobered in the next instant. "Did you hear that,

Granddad? I laughed right out loud. With Jack gone I wasn't sure I'd ever do that again."

"He'd want you to smile, laugh, get on with your life, Josie. He'd expect all of us to do that. It won't be easy, but it's what we must do.

"The fact that Michael went back to the oil works so quickly after the memorial service may have appeared cold and unfeeling to some people, but Michael knew he was better off keeping busy, rather than sitting and brooding. Besides, with Jack no longer in place as CEO, Michael is facing a mountain of work and increased responsibility."

"What about you, Granddad? Are you going to be all right here alone?"

"Of course. I've lived here with just Evelyn bustling around for many years now. I drop in at the oil works, go to my club and chat with friends, play a bit of golf, spend many enjoyable hours reading the classics. Don't worry about me, Josie. The pain of losing Jack won't ever disappear completely, but it *will* diminish in time. You'll see."

"I love you, Granddad."

"I love you, too, Princess. You pack your things and return to your apartment. I imagine you're in the midst of organizing some kind of charity event as usual."

"Yes," Josie said with a sigh. "You know that the interest from the trust allows me to donate my time to my favorite causes. Right now, though, I have no enthusiasm for tending to the details of a charity ball. I have an appointment next week in Tulsa with the manager of a band I'm supposed to be considering booking, but..."

Josie got to her feet and began to pace restlessly. "I want the sun to stop shining and the birds to stop chirping," she said, "and everyone to quit doing their usual routines. I feel as though I should stand in the middle of the hustle and bustle of Freemont Springs and scream, 'What's wrong with you people? Why are you going about your lives as you always have? Don't you know that Jack Wentworth is dead? Don't you know that—'" she stopped pacing and wrapped her hands around her elbows "'—that my beloved brother is never coming home again?'" Her whisper-soft voice was filled with tears.

"That's enough, Josie," Joseph said sternly. "You will *not* crumble under the weight of this tragedy. Are you listening to me? You're a Wentworth. Dry your tears, lift your chin and get on with your life. Go pack your belongings."

Josie nodded jerkily, dropped a kiss on her grandfather's cheek, then hurried from the room.

"You're a Wentworth, by God," Joseph said to the emptiness surrounding him.

He redirected his attention to the newspaper, but was unable to decipher the words through the mist of tears in his weary brown eyes.

Josie lived in the penthouse of a high-rise apartment building in an exclusive section of Freemont Springs. It was on the opposite side of the city from her grandfather's affluent neighborhood.

She'd chosen the location, she'd told Joseph, for

the simple reasons that she could afford it and the view from the floor-to-ceiling windows lining one entire wall of the enormous living room was dazzling.

When she'd moved in five years before, she'd totally redecorated, installing plush white carpeting throughout and having the walls painted a soothing salmon color. The furniture was big and marshmallow soft, in a mixture of white, salmon and mint green.

All the tables had clear glass tops on oak bases, including the dining-room table, which sat twenty people. There were only a few pictures on the walls, the ones she'd selected being large seascapes in muted tones.

The overall effect was open and airy and very inviting. The opulence was so subtle it was breathtaking. A guest had once remarked that she felt as though she was floating high above the city on a fluffy, comforting cloud while relaxing in Josie's living room.

Josie's bedroom was femininity personified. The king-size bed was covered in a white eyelet spread and dotted with varying sizes of white frilly pillows. The dresser and dressing table were oak, and a small round table with a white eyelet skirt was covered with a multitude of framed snapshots.

Josie kicked off her shoes after passing through the white-tiled foyer. She walked through the living room and headed straight for her bedroom, where she tossed her suitcase onto the bed.

She'd unpack later, she decided, wandering back

down the hallway. She glanced absently into the guest room, where a double bed was covered in a striped spread of salmon, mint green and white. More framed snapshots were on top of the oak dresser.

In the center of the living room, she stopped, sweeping her gaze over the place she called home.

Picture perfect, she thought, frowning. She'd spent thousands of dollars creating the exact atmosphere she wanted, with everything state-of-the-art.

When she entertained, her friends gushed profusely over her exquisite taste, some sighing in envy, not only about her home, but her life in general. The consensus among her social set was that Josie Wentworth had it all, including her pick of the most eligible bachelors in Freemont Springs and Tulsa.

"Picture-perfect apartment," Josie said aloud. "Picture-perfect life."

And it had been true, she supposed. She'd never questioned her right to possess what she had. It was her due—all part of being a Wentworth. She'd spent a thousand dollars for a crystal vase to set on the mantel above her gas log fireplace as casually as someone else might buy a loaf of bread.

That was what Wentworths did.

That was how Wentworths lived.

But somewhere in the midst of it all, she'd forgotten that there was the possibility that Wentworths might also die.

And now Jack was dead.

Josie hugged herself and stared up at the ceiling, willing herself not to give way to the tears that threatened yet again.

She was so tired of crying. So tired of the chill that gripped her heart in an iron fist. So tired of asking why, why, why her wonderful brother had died, and receiving only silence as an answer.

"Enough of this, Josie Wentworth," she said aloud. "Do something constructive and quit feeling sorry for yourself." She drew a steadying breath. "You are, after all, a Wentworth."

Her mail, she thought suddenly. When she'd made the decision to stay with her grandfather for a while, she'd requested that her mail be removed each day from the locked boxes in the lobby and held in the manager's office.

A dull session of paying bills and sorting through junk mail would provide a sense of normalcy to her life, she hoped. She'd call down and have the mail brought up right away.

Fifteen minutes later Josie entered the library that was off the dining room. She carried a medium-size box that had been delivered by the boy who worked in the small grocery store located in the corner of the lobby for the convenience of the tenants.

The library had a totally different decor than the remainder of the penthouse, and few people had ever been invited to enter the room.

During her burst of independence years before when she'd announced she was moving to her own apartment, she had not been as cocky and self-assured as the facade she'd presented to her family. Rather, she'd been scared to death to be stepping out into the world on her own. To leave the protective cocoon of her family had been exciting, but intertwined had been the stark emotion of fear.

So, she'd created a touch of her childhood home in her new residence. Her library was almost a replica of the one Joseph Wentworth spent many hours in at the estate.

As a little girl, she'd continually sought out her granddad in his special place, crawling into his lap while he sat in the massive, butter-soft leather chair behind his desk. Her granddad always stopped what he was doing to welcome her, making her feel special, important and very much loved.

Josie spent a great deal of time in her own library, allowing the warmth of the room to wrap itself around her like a comforting blanket. She, too, had a big wooden desk, a soft leather chair, a love seat of chocolate-colored leather and bookshelves filled to overflowing. Among the novels were the classics, a gift from her grandfather.

Josie set the box on the desk and lifted the flaps. She scooped out a pile of letters, flyers and magazines, set them on the blotter, then repeated the process. The towering stack of accumulated mail slipped to one side, sending several envelopes skittering to the floor.

She peered into the box and her breath caught. With shaking hands she removed a small box wrapped in brown paper. The upper left-hand corner stated that the package had been sent by Trey McGill.

Dear heaven, she thought, sinking into the chair

and placing the box gently on her lap. She'd forgotten all about this.

On the nightmare day Trey had gathered the family together to deliver the news of Jack's death, he'd taken Josie aside before leaving the house. He would, he'd said, see to it that Jack's personal effects were sent to her, to avoid upsetting her elderly granddad any further. Josie could then decide when to share Jack's belongings with her grandfather and Michael. Enveloped in a haze of misery, Josie had nodded absently in agreement, then promptly forgotten the conversation.

"Oh, dear," she whispered. "I'm not ready for this. I can't do this now."

But would opening the box be any less painful next week? Next month? Was there any real purpose in delaying seeing and touching her beloved Jack's personal belongings? No.

She took a pair of scissors from the top drawer of the desk and cut through the brown paper, brushing it away. After setting the scissors on the desk, she ever so slowly lifted the lid from the box and dropped it on the floor. She took a deep breath, then shifted her gaze to the contents of the package.

As though standing outside of herself and watching the solemn procedure, she reverently set Jack's wallet on the desk, followed by his dress watch, signet ring, keys, a pristine white handkerchief and a black plastic comb.

Josie frowned as she stared at the remaining three items, then snapped back to full attention.

There was a snapshot, a small, blue velvet box and

a stamped, addressed envelope. She lifted the items out and stood, allowing the now-empty box to fall to the floor. She crossed the room and sat on the love seat, placing the treasures on her lap.

She picked up the snapshot and stared at the smiling face of a pretty, young woman. Setting the photograph to one side, she opened the blue velvet box.

"Oh," she said, her eyes widening.

The box contained a beautiful emerald-cut diamond ring.

An engagement ring? she wondered, her mind racing. No. No way. Her love-'em-and-leave-'em, no-commitments brother was the last person on earth to plan on getting married.

But the lovely solitaire nestled in the velvet box certainly *looked* like an engagement ring.

Placing the ring box next to the snapshot of the smiling woman, Josie grasped the envelope with trembling fingers. She blinked away unwelcome tears as she saw Jack's familiar handwriting, big and bold and slashing across the paper.

"'Ms. Sabrina Jensen,'" she read aloud. "'Care of Max Carter, the Single C Ranch, Muskogee County, Oklahoma.'"

Josie stared at the letter, the ring, the snapshot, then back at the envelope.

Should she open it? Or should she simply mail it, assuming that was what Jack would have done if he'd been able to?

Think, Josie, she ordered herself. If Jack had fallen in love—incredible as the idea was—and planned to marry this Sabrina Jensen, then the Wentworth family should be gathering her into the fold, comforting her, hopefully easing some of her heartache by letting her know she wasn't alone in her grief.

But what if that wasn't the case? What if Jack had acted on impulse and was writing to Sabrina to end the relationship? The ring wasn't wrapped for mailing.

Then again, a man would want to slip an engagement ring on the finger of the woman he loved in person, not have her find the symbol of forever in her mailbox.

"I'm driving myself nuts," Josie muttered. "I'm just chasing my own thoughts in endless circles."

She pursed her lips, lifted her chin, opened the envelope and removed a single sheet of paper.

"'Dear Sabrina,'" she read, her voice sounding strange to her own ears. "'Our time together was magical. I need to see you, talk to you. I'll contact you as soon as I possibly can. J.'"

Josie dropped her hands heavily into her lap and leaned her head back, scowling at the ceiling.

Darn it, she thought. Jack needed to see and talk to Sabrina for what purpose? To ask her to marry him? Or to say it had been a great week, but see ya, toots? And the ring that was purchased in a sensual haze would be returned to the jeweler.

Josie lifted her head, reread the letter, then rose to her feet and began to pace the floor, the letter in one hand.

"What were you really saying to Sabrina, Jack?" she said to the empty room. "You're a lousy letter writer, do you know that, Jack Wentworth?"

Oh, what to do? she thought frantically, continuing her pacing. If Sabrina was to have been Jack's wife… But if Sabrina was only one more in Jack's endless stream of women…

"Okay, halt," she said, stopping in her tracks.

There was only one solution to this puzzle. She had to find Sabrina Jensen, talk to her, discover what feelings her brother had for this mysterious woman.

But until she knew the whole story, Josie decided, she would keep silent about the existence of Sabrina. Her dear grandfather's emotional plate had enough on it without adding the sorrowful possibility that Jack had fallen in love at long last only to be killed before he could marry his beloved.

Josie retrieved the envelope from the love seat and reread the address.

Well, Max Carter, whoever you are, she thought, *you're about to have a visitor.*

Chapter Two

It was another full day before Josie could leave Freemont Springs and put her plan to find Sabrina Jensen in motion.

Having no idea how long she would be away, she spent hours on the telephone, reassigning responsibilities for the forthcoming charity ball.

She then took on the task of determining just where in Muskogee County Max Carter's ranch, the Single C, was located.

After six wrong guesses as to whom to call and no help from the errors, she finally spoke with a member of the Cattlemen's Association, who located the Single C on a map. Josie wrote down extremely detailed directions, never having been one to have a natural sense of north and south or east and west.

It appeared, she thought, studying her sheet of paper, that she had about a hundred miles to drive from Freemont Springs to the Single C. She'd get up early the next morning and be on her way.

Packing was next on the agenda and proved to be a dilemma. With an empty suitcase on the bed, Josie stood in her walk-in closet, frowning as she tapped a fingertip against her chin.

What did one wear to visit an Oklahoma ranch? She didn't want to appear totally out of place in a designer suit and heels. Then again, shorts and a tank top were a tad too casual. After all, she hoped to find Sabrina Jensen at the ranch and have a very serious discussion with her as to the status of her relationship with Jack.

If, heaven forbid, Sabrina had moved on, Josie would have to travel to wherever Max Carter directed her to go next.

Max Carter, Josie mused, pulling a pair of designer jeans from a hanger. Just who was he to Sabrina? Her father? Grandfather? Uncle? She envisioned him as an older man, a weathered rancher with leathery skin and bowed legs. A crotchety good old boy with a blustery demeanor and a heart of gold.

Oh, and he was a confirmed bachelor, Josie imagined, evidenced by the name of his ranch. No, no, he had been very much in love years and years ago, but his lady had run off with a dandy from the city. Max had then devoted his life to his land, having vowed never to love again.

"Poor, dear old Max," Josie said with a shake of her head.

Settling on a variety of clothes, she left space in

the suitcase for her cosmetic bag, which she'd tuck in the next morning.

Once again she made arrangements for her mail to be collected, called the cleaning service to tell them to proceed on schedule with the upkeep of her apartment, then left a message on Michael's answering machine. She told her brother she was going on a trip and they should plan to have dinner together when she returned.

She was ready to go, she realized, except for the biggy—the dreaded task of informing her grandfather that she was leaving Freemont Springs for an undetermined length of time.

Josie sank onto the sofa in the living room and stared into space.

From the time she was old enough to talk, Joseph Wentworth had possessed an uncanny ability to know when his granddaughter wasn't telling the truth. It was very annoying.

How on earth was she going to bluff her way through the explanation for her sudden exodus without divulging to Joseph the real reason for her trip?

Somehow she had to pull this off. It would be unkind to tell her grandfather about Sabrina without knowing the true place the woman had had in Jack's life.

If, indeed Jack had been planning to marry Sabrina Jensen, Joseph would want to spend time with the young woman talking about Jack, sharing stories and memories. Sabrina would be a most welcome link to Jack, a living, breathing, loving connection.

No, her granddad mustn't know about Sabrina at this point. He didn't deserve another disappointment.

"So?" Josie said aloud. "How do I explain where I'm going and why I'm going there without spilling the beans to Granddad?"

First, she thought, she wouldn't make her announcement in person. She'd never figured out how her granddad always knew when she was fibbing, but it was probably telegraphed in her eyes. No, she wouldn't run the risk of going to the estate to talk to her grandfather.

"Wing it," she said, then reached for the telephone.

She punched in the familiar numbers and seconds later greeted Evvie. Within moments after that, she heard her grandfather's voice.

"Hello, Josie," he said.

"Hi, Granddad. How are you?"

"Fairly well. What can I do for you this evening, Princess?"

"Me? Well, I called to tell you I've decided to go on a trip. I'm leaving first thing in the morning. I'm driving to...wherever I end up driving to. I'm not certain when I'll be back, but I'll keep in touch, so there's no reason for you to worry. Okay? Bye, Granddad."

"Hold it, young lady," Joseph said sternly.

Josie grimaced. "Yes?"

"You're chattering like a magpie. Just slow down and tell me why you've suddenly decided to leave Freemont Springs, destination unknown."

"I need...I need to get away, get my emotions

under control again. I can't plan a charity ball in the state I'm in. I have...yes, I have unfinished emotional business about Jack I have to deal with."

There, Josie thought. Not bad. She hadn't really lied—just sort of.

"I see," Joseph said. "Well, that makes sense, I guess."

It did? Fancy that. She was definitely on a roll.

"However," Joseph said, "I've taught you that you can't run from your troubles, Josie. You have to square off against them, stand steady and tall."

"I realize that, Granddad, but I think some quiet time away is just the ticket for my gloomy state of mind." She shrugged. "If it doesn't work, I'll turn around and come home."

"Yes, all right. Do you at least know what direction you're headed in?"

"I thought I'd start out toward the Muskogee area."

"That's pretty country." He paused. "You'll telephone me?"

"Yes, of course. Please don't fret about me, Granddad. I'll drive very carefully. I love you. Take good care of yourself while I'm away."

"Yes, I will. I love you, too, Princess. I hope you find what you're looking for on this journey."

"So do I. More than you know. Good night, Granddad."

"Good night, Princess."

Josie replaced the receiver slowly, then sighed.

Oh, Jack, she thought. *Who is Sabrina Jensen? Did you love her, plan to marry her? Did you ac-*

tually fall in love, my dear brother? If that's true, I'll find Sabrina, and welcome her into our family. I promise you that.

Josie got to her feet, suddenly weary from her busy day.

Before she slipped between the cool satin sheets on her bed, she tucked the letter and the blue velvet box containing the diamond ring into her purse.

The next morning Josie awoke feeling almost lighthearted. There was still a dark cloud of despair hovering over her that would send a chill coursing through her when she least expected it. But in the light of this new day, she at least had a sense of purpose, a mission, instead of focusing entirely on the loss of her brother.

She showered, dressed in snug jeans, a red sweater and white tennis shoes, then had a cup of hot tea.

A short time later she placed her suitcase in the trunk of her pearly blue BMW and drove out of the underground garage.

Her first stop, she decided, would be her favorite bakery. She would indulge in a bag of cinnamon doughnut holes to snack on as she drove. The calorie-laden purchase would be a special treat to herself.

The bakery was two blocks away and Josie found a parking spot right in front. Named simply Freemont Springs Bakery, it was owned by Millie Williams and Bea Hansen, two women in their late fifties. They were excellent pastry chefs, were friendly and outgoing, and enjoyed a juicy tidbit of gossip even more than they did their delicious culinary offerings.

A bell tinkled merrily over the door as Josie entered the store and inhaled the mouth-watering aroma of baked goods. Both Bea and Millie appeared instantly from the rear.

"Josie Wentworth," Bea said. "How wonderful to see you." She frowned. "Oh, my darling girl, we are so sorry about Jack. I still find it hard to believe that he's..." She shook her head. "Our condolences, dear."

"Thank you," Josie said, managing to produce a small smile.

"I remember when Jack was a boy," Millie said. "He went everywhere on his bicycle, with no thought to the distance. He used to pedal from your grandfather's house all the way over here to have cream puffs. How that boy loved those cream puffs."

"He still does...did," Josie said quietly. "Cream puffs with chocolate filling."

"Oh, yes, always chocolate inside," Millie said. "We worked out a trade. He'd wash the front window and he'd get three chocolate-filled cream puffs." She frowned. "This must be such a difficult time for you and your family, Josie."

"Yes. Yes, it is," Josie said. "Well, I mustn't stand here chatting. I'd like a dozen cinnamon doughnut holes, please."

"Sharing breakfast with someone special?" Bea asked as Millie moved around her to fetch Josie's order.

"No." Josie smiled. "I'm going on a road trip and I plan to nibble on the way."

"Oh?" Bea leaned slightly forward. "Where are you going, dear?"

Josie shrugged. "Wherever the road takes me. I need some time alone right now. I'll start off down Muskogee way and see what unfolds."

"Isn't that dangerous?" Millie said, plopping doughnut holes in a waxed bag. "A woman alone on the road?"

"Not if I use common sense," Josie said. "I'll be fine."

"One dozen cinnamon doughnut holes," Millie said, placing the bag on top of the tall, glass-fronted display case.

Josie opened her purse at the same time she lifted it up to set it on the counter. The bottom of the tapestry purse caught on the edge of the counter and pitched forward, spilling some of the contents.

"Oh, drat," Josie said. "I'm sorry."

She began to scoop her belongings back into the purse. Bea bent down to retrieve something from the floor. Josie groaned inwardly when Bea straightened again with the blue velvet ring box in her hand.

"Land's sake," Bea declared, beaming. "Is this what I think it is? Is there a ring in this pretty box, Josie Wentworth? An engagement ring?"

"Oh, well, I..." Josie started.

"You're going off to decide if you want to marry him," Millie said, clasping her hands beneath her chin.

"Him who?" Josie frowned.

"That is so romantic." Bea gave a wistful sigh.

"Here I thought you were taking private time to deal with your grief over Jack. Who is he, Josie?"

Good grief, Josie thought. Whatever she said to these two lovable ladies might as well be announced on the six-o'clock news. She certainly couldn't tell them the truth about that blue velvet box. Well, *they* didn't possess her grandfather's ability to know when she was telling tall tales.

Go for it, Josie.

"He's... Oh, my." Josie placed one hand over her heart and smiled as she stared into space.

"Yes?" Bea and Millie said in unison.

"You don't know him," Josie said, looking at the pair again. "He's from Texas. He has a zillion oil wells in Texas, you see, and had flown over to Tulsa for a charity auction that I attended." She sighed wistfully. "He just swept me off my feet, sent dozens of roses to my hotel room, wined and dined me until my head was in the clouds. It was all so-o-o romantic. He proposed to me under the stars."

"Oh, my," Bea said, "isn't that enchanting?"

"He proposed," Millie prompted. "And you said?"

"Yes, well, I have to contemplate, weigh and measure," Josie said. "Do I want to marry him? Leave Oklahoma?" She reached across the counter, plucked the ring box from Bea's hand, then popped it back into her purse. "So many questions. I must be off, dear friends. My mind is a muddle. How much do I owe you for my snack?"

Bea told her, then asked, "You will tell us what you decide to do, won't you?"

"Of course." Josie removed her wallet from her purse. "I wouldn't dream of keeping something of this magnitude from you. Heavens, I wonder if there's a bakery as fine as yours in Texas? A future without yummy doughnut holes would be very bleak."

"We could mail them to you." Millie said.

"There's a thought." Josie smiled brightly. She paid for her purchase and headed quickly for the door.

"Ta-ta," she said.

"Have a good trip, dear," Millie called.

As Josie drove away from the bakery, she blew a puff of air up over her flushed face.

That encounter, she thought, had not been an auspicious beginning to her new role as detective. Imagine, spilling the evidence all over the floor. Cripes.

She'd better get her act together before she took on old Max. The rancher probably had a sixth sense about people, borne of living and surviving on the land.

She'd have to be friendly and sincere to get past Max Carter and close to Sabrina Jensen—if Sabrina was still at the Single C Ranch. Fine. No problem. She was a friendly and sincere person. This mission would be a piece of cake.

"No, it will be a doughnut hole," Josie said, then popped one into her mouth. "Mmm."

After a quick stop at a convenience store for a soft drink to accompany the pastries, Josie joined the multitude of other drivers on the busy city streets.

Escaping at last from the heavy traffic when she reached the interstate, Josie pressed harder on the gas pedal. The expensive car responded instantly. She wriggled deeper into the bucket seat and settled in to enjoy the drive and the lush scenery that stretched as far as the eye could see on both sides of the highway.

There were sections of towering pine trees that made her think of the holidays, which were creeping closer. A Christmas without Jack, she thought. Yes, there'd been a few times in the past when he'd been unable to be home on the special day due to an assignment for the SEABEES. But they'd left the tree up at their grandfather's house and reenacted the event for Jack when he finally arrived, complete with a turkey dinner with all the trimmings.

But this year, and all the years to come, Jack wouldn't celebrate Christmas with his family. Not Christmas or his birthday or—

"Stop it, Josie," she whispered, as she felt tears sting her eyes.

She mustn't dwell on who she had lost. She had to concentrate on who she was hoping to find—Sabrina Jensen, a woman who might be the one who had finally captured the elusive heart of Jack Wentworth.

With a decisive nod Josie mentally pushed aside her sorrowful thoughts of a future without Jack. She concentrated on the traffic, as well as the beauty of nature within her view. In addition to the pines, there were hickory and oak trees, their leaves a kaleidoscope of vibrant fall colors.

She suddenly remembered the long walks in the

woods with Granddad, Jack and Michael. Every year, Joseph Wentworth would gather the children and take them for a leisurely stroll through the beautiful trees that boasted leaves touched by nature's paintbrush. The breeze would hum through the drying leaves on the branches above, and small feet would crunch the carpet of leaves below.

"Listen," Joseph would always say to his three young charges. "That's the song of autumn you're hearing. Once a year the colored leaves sing a special, magical melody."

Josie had been enthralled. She'd start watching the leaves for weeks before they began to turn, waiting with tingling anticipation for the traditional walk in the woods and the magical music.

"Granddad—" she'd finally yell, running through the house in search of him "—it's time! It's time! We've got to go to the woods to hear the song of autumn!"

A soft smile formed on Josie's lips as she glanced again at the gorgeous trees along the road.

Beautiful memories. Her grandfather had given her so much as a child, not just material things but gifts of the heart, as well. Granted, he'd spoiled her rotten, but she'd always known she was deeply loved.

Joseph had been a hard taskmaster, too. He'd been very strict about grades at school, accepting nothing less than perfection from the three Wentworth offspring. If one of them struggled with a subject, playtime would be forfeited for grueling hours with a tutor.

Josie and Jack had taken their grandfather's somewhat heavy-handed authority in stride. Michael, however, had rebelled during his teens, resulting in frequent shouting matches with Joseph.

Even though Michael was now twenty-seven, the pair still locked horns with disturbing regularity.

He was the head of the family, Joseph would roar, and his orders were to be followed without question. Michael's response was usually an angry exit, complete with a slammed door. He would disappear for several hours, not returning until his temper had cooled.

Josie pulled herself from her rambling thoughts as she saw a sign at the edge of the highway announcing that the exit ramp for Muskogee was five miles ahead.

She would, she knew, have to locate the Single C Ranch by following the directions she'd written on the paper tucked carefully next to her in the bucket seat. That was definitely a daunting thought. The idea of using a map she herself had drawn did not instill great confidence that she'd reach the desired destination.

Think positively, she told herself. She would find the Single C, Max Carter *and* Sabrina Jensen. One. Two. Three.

Josie left the interstate at the designated exit and felt a surge of excitement.

Every mile covered brought her closer to Sabrina. Within the next hour or so they might very well be face-to-face and chatting like sisters, she and the woman her dear brother Jack, it appeared, had loved and planned to marry.

Chapter Three

Nearly three hours later a very frustrated and stressed-to-the-maximum Josie glowered at the iron archway that spelled out "Single C" above the entrance to a dirt road.

She had managed, somehow, to get hopelessly lost despite her lengthy detailed map. Now she was hungry, thirsty and irritated beyond belief.

"You'd better not give me any grief, Max Carter," Josie muttered, pressing on the gas pedal. "I'm not in the mood, mister."

The dirt road was filled with ruts, forcing Josie to drive at a crawl, which did nothing for her totally deteriorated frame of mind. Dust billowed up and over the car like a giant marshmallow, leaving a gritty coating on the shiny surface.

She finally emerged from the dusty cocoon as she

reached a narrow strip of gravel spread in front of a medium-size, one-story wood house. It was white with brown trim that was in need of paint in places.

A porch ran across the entire front of the structure. It was bare, without even one chair to sit on to enjoy an evening breeze.

Three wide steps leading to the porch sagged in the middle. Weeds were the landscaping of choice between the gravel and the house.

"Charming," Josie said dryly. "Old Max obviously isn't into tender lovin' care regarding his home."

Josie turned off the ignition, then flipped the visor down to check her appearance in the mirror. She ran a comb through her hair, applied fresh lipstick and told herself to smile.

Friendly and sincere, she mentally repeated like a mantra. Friendly and sincere.

She got out of the car, flung the strap of her purse over one shoulder, then straightened the waistband of her sweater. After taking a deep, steadying breath, she started toward the house, weaving her way among the weeds that grew through the cracks in the sidewalk leading to the front steps.

The steps themselves she tested cautiously, not certain the sagging boards would support her weight. Finally arriving safely at the front door, she lifted her chin to a determined tilt and knocked firmly.

When there was no response, she knocked again, straining to hear any indication that someone was inside and planning to answer the summons.

Darn it, she thought with a sigh. There was obviously no one in the house. Well, that made sense, she supposed. This was a working ranch. Old Max wouldn't be hanging out in his living room in the middle of the afternoon watching soap operas on television. There was not, it would seem, a Mrs. Max.

Josie made her way back down the steps, along the sidewalk and headed for the rear of the house. She saw a bright red barn gleaming in the afternoon sun, pristine white corral fences and several small dark brown buildings.

Now there, she mused, was tender lovin' care. Max Carter apparently put his money and energy into everything but his house.

She'd read about early settlers living in tents or sod huts while constructing huge barns. Max must be of that mind-set. It seemed everything on his ranch came before the maintenance of his home.

Whatever, she thought, with a shrug.

Josie passed a corral where a horse munched lazily on some scrub grass. She had yet to see a human being and so she kept going in the direction of the barn. When she was twenty feet in front of the wide open doors, a man appeared.

Max, she thought. He looked exactly as she'd imagined him. Somewhere in his seventies, small and wiry, his skin tanned and weathered.

He even had bowed legs!

The cowboy hat he wore had seen better days, and gray stubble covered his cheeks and chin, indicating he hadn't bothered to shave that morning.

Josie quickened her step, smiling and extending her hand as she stopped in front of the man.

"Good afternoon, Mr. Carter," she said brightly. "This is such a pleasure. I'm Josie Wentworth from Freemont Springs."

The man frowned, looked at Josie's hand, her face, then gave her hand a firm, brisk shake.

"I've come all this way to speak to you about a personal matter of utmost importance," she went on, still smiling to beat the band. "Is there somewhere we could sit down together and have a private conversation, Max? May I call you Max?"

The man lifted one shoulder in a shrug.

"You can call me Max if you want to," he said, his voice gravelly.

"Splendid, and I'm Josie. So! Shall we go into the house where we won't be disturbed?"

"Well, now," he said, running one hand over his beard-stubbled chin, "I don't believe that would be proper."

"For us to be alone together in the house?" she said, raising her eyebrows. "My, my, aren't you the old-fashioned gentleman. That is so sweet, so refreshing. Would you be more comfortable if we left the door open?"

"Nope."

"Oh," Josie said, frowning. "Well, we could carry two chairs to the front porch. How's that?"

"Nope."

"Max, please," she said with a sigh of exasperation. "Pick a place. Okay? I'll follow you anywhere.

It's vitally important that I speak to you about this private and personal matter."

"There now, you see," he said. "That's where we're running into trouble. It wouldn't be right and fittin' for me to be talking about a private and personal matter with you, Josie."

Josie planted her hands on her hips. "Why on earth not?"

A slow grin crept onto the old cowboy's face. "Because I'm not Max Carter."

"What!" Josie said, nearly shrieking. "You're not Max? Then why did you say you were?"

"Never did. You asked me if you could call me Max, and I figured I didn't mind what you called me. The name's Rusty, though."

"Oh, good grief," Josie said, squeezing the bridge of her nose for a moment. "I don't believe this."

She took a deep breath, willing the frustration that was bordering on anger back under control.

"Okay. Fine," she said. "Let's start over...Rusty. I'm Josie Wentworth from Freemont Springs, and I've come to speak with Mr. Max Carter of the Single C Ranch. Is he available?"

"Depends on what you mean by available. Max is a couple miles north, pulling out a dead tree stump. Don't expect him in for a spell."

"I see. Well, do you have a vehicle you could drive to take me to where he is?"

"Nope."

"I don't suppose he carries a cell phone in his boot," Josie said dismally.

"Nope."

"Look, how would you reach him if there was an emergency here at the barn?"

"I reckon I'd hitch up the wagon and go out there and fetch him."

"But you said you didn't have a vehicle to... Never mind."

"Thought you meant a truck or Jeep or something of that nature."

"Rusty," Josie said, striving desperately for patience, "would you please get the wagon you were speaking of and take me to wherever Max Carter is doing whatever he is doing with the dead tree?"

"I guess I could do that."

"Thank you."

"Then again, Max might not take kindly to being interrupted. You say it's important, this private and personal matter?"

"*Very* important."

"Well, it's your hide if you're trying to sell him something. Max won't be losing any work time yapping with a saleslady, even one as pretty as you."

"I solemnly swear to you that I'm not selling anything, Rusty."

The old man nodded. "Then I guess I'll go get the wagon hitched up."

"Thank you," she said, managing to produce a pleasant—albeit phony—smile. "I'm most appreciative of your efforts on my behalf."

Josie rolled her eyes heavenward as Rusty turned and ambled back into the barn, moving so slowly she decided he might very well fall asleep on his feet.

She folded her arms over her breasts, tapped one foot and waited.

And waited.

When the last ounce of patience she possessed was gone, she started toward the entrance of the barn—just as Rusty reappeared leading a plodding horse by the reins.

Look at that beast, Josie thought, aware of a hint of hysteria creeping in around the edges of her brain. The horse must have come sailing over on the *Mayflower* at the same time Rusty did.

Behind the swaybacked horse was a rickety wagon with a springboard seat. Rusty climbed up on the seat, then adjusted the reins.

"You coming?" he said.

"Yes, of course," Josie said.

She hiked the strap of her purse higher on her shoulder and marched to the side of the wagon. After two failed attempts, she finally managed to plunk herself on the hard board, feeling like a toddler who'd just crawled up the stairs.

"All set?" Rusty said.

"Yes. Thank you," she answered, then folded her hands primly in her lap.

"Yo. Yip," Rusty said, flicking the reins on the horse's wide back.

The animal took off like a shot.

"Oh, no!" Josie screamed.

She nearly fell into the wagon bed, saving herself at the last second by gripping the front edge of the seat.

"Slow down!" she hollered, as they barreled out of the barnyard.

"Can't," Rusty yelled. "This horse has two speeds—half-dead slow and full steam ahead. He gets you where you want to go, though, no doubt about it."

"Why me, why me?" Josie murmured, her eyes wide with terror. "Oh, good night. Oh, my gosh. Oh. Oh. Whoa. Whoa. Oh."

She squeezed her eyes closed and hung on for dear life, trying to ignore the pain as her bottom bounced on the unyielding board.

After what seemed like an eternity, Rusty bellowed a hearty "Whoa." The horse came to such an abrupt halt that Josie nearly toppled forward onto the sweaty beast.

She opened her eyes slowly, taking a deep, steadying breath in the process.

She blinked, then closed her eyes again, wild thoughts racing through her mind.

Something had jarred loose in her brain during the ride from hell, she thought frantically. She'd just seen the most gorgeous, blatantly masculine, ruggedly handsome man her imagination could conjure up. Where in her subconscious had *he* been hiding?

With her eyes still shut, she could visualize in crystal clarity every inch of his six-foot body.

He had shaggy black hair creeping below a sweat-stained Stetson, ebony eyes, tanned skin, wide shoulders and long, muscular legs, lovingly hugged by faded jeans.

Those jeans were resting low on narrow hips below a bare chest covered in moist, dark curls. Taut muscles accentuated his perfectly proportioned arms. One large hand was wrapped around the handle of a shovel that was planted on the ground next to an enormous tree stump that was lying on its side.

Gracious, Josie thought, what a delicious image. Well, enough was enough. She was settled down now with everything back in working order. She was going to open her eyes again, then ask Rusty how she could find Max Carter out here in the…wherever he'd brought her.

Josie opened her eyes and her breath caught.

He was still there. The masculinity-personified hunk-of-stuff was still standing there. And he was not a happy person. His eyebrows were drawn together in a fierce frown, making a dark slash above his straight blade of a nose.

"Howdy there, Max," Rusty said. "You got company come to call. This lady is Josie Wentworth from over Freemont Springs way. She has private and personal business to discuss with you."

This was Max Carter? Josie swallowed a bubble of nearly hysterical laughter. He wasn't a mirage? He was real? He was Max?

"That a fact?" Max said, still glowering at her.

Oh, that voice, Josie thought. So deep, rumbly, befitting his size. The man didn't quit. He just got better and better.

"Just what is it you want, Ms. Wentworth?" Max said.

"You can call her Josie." Rusty chuckled. "No

telling what she might call *you.* She picks a name and sticks it on you."

"Mmm," Max said. "Well? I'm a busy man... Josie. Speak, or go away."

Get a grip, Josie Wentworth, she ordered herself. This was Max Carter, the link to Sabrina Jensen. He was obviously long on sex appeal and very short on patience and manners.

She was going to have to make a good first impression, because she had a sneaking suspicion she was only going to get one shot at speaking with Max Carter.

"I realize your time..." she started, then stopped and cleared her throat as she heard the squeaky sound of her voice. "I realize your time is valuable, Mr. Carter. If we could speak privately, I'll be brief and to the point. Oh, and I hereby swear that I'm not selling anything. It's extremely important. Might we have a few minutes alone? Please?"

Max sighed.

Damn, he thought. He'd been a word away from telling Rusty to take Ms. Fancy Britches Wentworth back up to the house and send her packing. There was nothing—absolutely nothing—private and personal he could possibly have to discuss with this woman.

This extremely beautiful woman.

Here he was covered in mud, muck and sweat, having strained every muscle in his body to the point of bone-deep pain, and the next thing he knew he was staring at one of the most delectable women he'd ever seen.

The sun created a halo around her shiny auburn hair. The breeze sifted through it, swinging it back and forth, beckoning to his fingers to join in.

Her features were delicate, her eyes big and brown, reminding him of a fawn, and her skin was why the phrase "peaches and cream" had been invented.

And her lips? Lord, those lips. They had to be the most kissable in the state of Oklahoma.

Full breasts were pushing against her tight little sweater and...

Max's frown deepened.

He took in more details: the designer jeans, the manicured and polished nails, the obvious quality of her tapestry-and-leather purse.

Quickly he came out of the sensual spell Josie Wentworth had cast over him, and ignored the coiling heat he could feel tightening low in his belly as he stared at her.

Josie Wentworth was money. And whatever she wanted to talk to him about he wasn't interested, not one damn bit.

Oh, yeah, he'd been ready to send her on her way.

But then?

Then she'd drawn a shuddering little breath and said, "Please?" in a voice ringing with an unnamed emotion that had been his undoing.

Damn.

"Ten minutes," he said gruffly. "You'd better talk fast, Josie Wentworth, because that's all I can spare you to deliver your spiel."

"Oh, thank you, Mr.... Max," she said.

"Mmm," he said, tugging his Stetson low on his forehead.

"You want me to hang around and take her back up front, boss?" Rusty said.

"No," Max replied. "You go on. I'm going to have to come in to get some dynamite. I got the tree stump out, but there's a big boulder down in that hole that I want gone before we plow this section. I'll drive her back in the truck."

"Gotcha," Rusty said.

Josie wiggled to the edge of the wooden seat, then jumped to the ground. Rusty clucked to the horse and the animal once again took off at full speed.

"Weird horse," Josie said, staring after Rusty and the beast.

"He has a mind of his own, but then all of us here on the Single C do." Max wrapped both hands around the shovel handle and propped one booted foot on top of the blade. "Your clock is ticking."

"Yes, well, is there somewhere we could go to be a bit more comfortable? You know, perhaps sit down?"

"Do you expect me to serve tea and crumpets, too?"

"There's no call for being grumpy and rude," Josie said, planting her hands on her hips. "It was a perfectly reasonable question."

"Yeah, right," Max said, a very sarcastic edge to his voice.

He pulled the shovel from the dirt, placed it in the back of the truck, then untied a thick rope from the tree stump and a hitch, and tossed the rope in after the shovel. He then let down the tailgate of the truck and leaned on the edge.

"Your throne, madam," he said with a sweep of one arm. "And I repeat, your clock is ticking."

Josie sighed and walked to the tailgate. She stared at it, wondering how on earth she was going to crawl up onto it in a ladylike manner.

"Oh, for cripe's sake," Max said, pushing his Stetson up with his thumb.

Josie gasped as Max grasped her around the waist and lifted her up onto the tailgate as though she weighed no more than a feather pillow.

Instead of shifting away, Max flattened one hand on either side of her and looked directly into her eyes.

"What's on your mind, Josie?" he said quietly, his voice very deep and very, *very* rumbly.

Mind? she thought hazily. What mind? Dear heaven, she couldn't breathe, let alone think. Max Carter's dark eyes were mesmerizing, making it impossible for her to tear her gaze from his.

He had her trapped by his arms and body; trapped in an enclosure of potent masculinity that was sending currents of heat shooting through her like rockets on the Fourth of July.

Move, Carter, Max ordered himself. What in the hell did he think he was doing? He was going up in flames—hot, painful flames.

He was so close to Josie that if he inched forward he could capture those delectable lips with his mouth and taste her, inhale even more of her flowery cologne.

Lord, she was tempting.

She was sweet ice cream on a hot summer day, just waiting to be savored slowly, a little enticing bit at a time.

Josie Wentworth was... Wentworth? his mind echoed suddenly. As in, Wentworth Oil Works? *The* Wentworths of Oklahoma? Ah, hell, that would explain her fancy jeans, the stylish purse, the professional polish on her nails and... Wentworth. Megabucks. Right out of the slice of society he despised.

"Wentworth Oil," he said, straightening and taking a step backward.

"Who?" Josie said, then blinked. "Oh. Wentworth Oil. Well, I'm not here representing my family's enterprise. In fact, none of them even know about you or this visit. They believe I'm taking some private time alone with no particular destination for an undetermined length of time."

"But you *are* one of *those* Wentworths."

Josie frowned. "Yes, but you don't have to make it sound like a disease. I've come on personal business. I'm attempting to locate Sabrina Jensen."

"My cousin Sabrina?" Max said, surprise evident on his face. "Why? What could you possibly want with Sabrina?"

Sabrina was Max's cousin? Josie thought. Well, wasn't *that* nice. She wasn't his wife or lover or lady friend. Sabrina was Max's cousin. Why did that make her feel so bubbly, so relieved, so—?

Because of Jack. Of course, that was it. It would be just awful if Jack had fallen in love at long last, only to lose his heart to a woman who belonged to someone else.

"Come on, Josie," Max said, folding his arms over his chest. "Spill it. What do you want with Sabrina?"

"Do you know where she is?"

"Back up. *I* asked *you* a question."

"All right," Josie said with a sigh. "My brother, Jack, was killed recently while on a special assignment with the State Department. Among his personal effects I found a letter from Jack to Sabrina. It was addressed to her in care of you at the Single C ranch."

"Let me guess," Max said. "You read the letter. You just helped yourself, opened it and read it."

"Well, yes, because I needed to know—"

"Have you ever heard of privacy?" Max interrupted. "Of respecting other people's belongings? That letter was Sabrina's, not yours. What right did you have to read it?" He shook his head. "Oh, wait a minute. You're a Wentworth of the millionaire jet set. You do whatever you damn well please, don't you?"

"You don't understand," Josie said, her voice rising. "There was a blue velvet box holding an engagement ring in Jack's belongings, too. I have to find out if he intended to ask Sabrina to marry him."

"What difference does it make?" Max shouted. "The man is dead."

Josie shivered from the pain of the stark reality of Max's shouted words, then she allowed her anger to have full rein.

"Because, you dolt," she said, hopping down off the tailgate, "if Jack *was* in love with Sabrina and intended to ask her to marry him, then she is, in my opinion, a member of our family. She could bring a great deal of comfort to me, to my grandfather and—"

"Listen to yourself." Max leaned toward her, yelling close to her face. "All you're thinking about is what *you* want. Have you given one thought to Sabrina's feelings, what her wishes might be? Hell, no. A Wentworth has spoken, so by God, that's how it's going to be.

"Well, I've got news for you, lady." Max snatched his shirt off the side of the truck bed and yanked it on, not bothering to fasten the snaps or tuck it into his jeans. "*I* respect Sabrina's privacy. If she has anything to say to you, she'll decide that on her own."

Josie narrowed her eyes. "You're not going to tell me where she is, are you?"

"Not in this lifetime."

Josie settled the strap of her purse higher on her shoulder and began to back up.

"You're despicable, do you know that, Max Carter?" she said. "You're narrow-minded and stubborn and... I'm attempting to do the right and decent thing here and you're..."

"Watch where you're going!"

But it was too late.

With a scream that sliced through the air, Josie toppled backward into the hole created by the removal of the tree stump.

Max swore and rushed forward, his heart thundering as he looked down to see Josie lying still with her eyes closed, the back of her head on the edge of the solid, menacing boulder.

Chapter Four

"Come on, beautiful, open your eyes. It's time to wake up now."

Deep in a dark tunnel that was cool and quiet and soothing, she heard the insistent voice of a man who was urging her to leave her lovely haven.

No, she thought. *Leave me alone. I'm sleeping, sleeping, sleeping....*

"You moved a bit. I know you can hear me. Let me see those big brown, fawn eyes of yours."

Fawn eyes? she thought. Did *she* have eyes like a fawn? Brown eyes? Her eyes were— Oh, what difference did it make? She was sleeping, not worrying about the color of her eyes. Besides, she knew her eyes were...were... *What color were her eyes?*

She jerked, as somewhere in the dark tunnel the realization that she had no idea what color her eyes were jolted her from the peaceful place. Pain radiated instantly through her head like a hot poker, and she moaned as she lifted her lashes slowly.

"There she is," the man said. "How's your head feeling?"

"Hurts," she said, closing her eyes again.

"Oh, no, you don't. You've been fading in and out on me for the past fifteen minutes, and now you're finally talking. Stay awake. I know your head hurts, but you have to stay with me here."

She tried again, squinting against the pain as she moved her head just enough to see the man who was speaking to her.

Ruggedly handsome, she thought foggily. Nice, very nice, but that was beside the point.

"Who are you?" she said, her voice hardly more than a whisper.

The man frowned. "What?"

"Who are you? Where am I?" Her eyes flew all the way open and she pressed both hands to her head. "Oh, dear God, who am *I*?"

"Uh-oh," an older man said, peering over the hunk's shoulder at her. She was lying on a sofa.

"Take it easy," the younger man said. He was hunkered down next to the sofa. "There's a doctor on the way to have a look at you. You fell into a hole and hit your head on a rock. Do you remember that?"

"No. No, I don't remember anything," she said, panic rushing through her. She struggled to sit up, only to clutch her head more tightly and fall back against the pillow. "My head. I can't think. I... Why don't I know who I am? Who are you?"

"Shh. Relax. Okay?" he said. "You had a nasty bump on the head, that's all. Things will become clear in a few minutes. Just rest and wait for that headache to ease some. You're going to be just fine."

"But—"

"I hear a car. That'll be the doctor. Don't move. Just lie still."

Max planted his hands on his thighs and pushed himself to his feet. He strode across the room and headed for the front door.

Holy hell, he thought, dragging one hand through his hair. Josie didn't remember who she was, who *he* was, where she was. She'd hit her head on that damn boulder and... Did she have a full-blown case of amnesia? Could a knock on the head like she'd had totally erase a person's memory?

Max flung open the front door, grabbed the arm of the man who stood on the porch, then literally hauled him into the house.

"Cripe's, Carter," the man said. "Tear my arm off."

"Oh, sorry, Jeff. I... Damn."

"I've never seen you so shook up," Jeff said. "You said on the phone that you had a woman visitor who fell, hit her head and was unconscious. That's not great news, but it's not something to come unglued about."

Max glowered at his friend, who was a few years older. Jeff Wilson was short and slightly overweight.

He'd gone to medical school, then returned to his roots to fulfill his dream of becoming an old-fashioned country doctor. He was married and had three children, with another one on the way.

"She woke up," Max said gruffly.

"Well, that's good," Jeff said, nodding. "She probably has a helluva headache, too."

"Yeah, she does, but—" Max glanced back toward the sofa and lowered his voice "—she can't remember anything. Nothing. She doesn't even know who *she* is, let alone who *I* am."

"Whew. She really took a pop on the bean, huh? I'll have a look at her. Sounds like she has retrograde amnesia, though."

"How long will it last?"

Jeff shrugged. "No telling. It varies from person to person. It's rather frightening for the patient. I mean, think about it. Her mind is a blank blackboard. That can be scary as hell. But I'm getting ahead of myself. Let me examine her and draw my own conclusions. What's the lady's name?"

"Josie."

"Okay. You go outside, Carter, and get your act together. If Josie does have amnesia, she's going to need a lot of calm reassurance that her memory will return. At the moment you're worthless."

"Yeah, well, hell," Max said, then went out the front door.

He began to pace the length of the porch, his strides heavy. Rusty appeared minutes later.

"Jeff threw me out," Rusty said. "Lordy, boss, that pretty little gal can't remember anything."

"I'm aware of that, Rusty," Max said, shooting him a dark glare. He shook his head. "Man, I don't need this. Josie had better get her memory back fast, that's for damn sure."

"What if she doesn't?"

Max stopped his trek. "Don't you have something to do in the barn?"

"I'm gone." Rusty raised both hands, then hustled off.

As Rusty disappeared around the side of the house, Max resisted the urge to punch the porch beam, deciding he'd probably bring the entire thing crashing down around him.

Then again, maybe that wasn't such a bad idea, he thought. He might get whopped on the head and suffer a comforting case of amnesia. Then he could just wander here and there on the Single C and be oblivious to the dilemma he was now facing regarding Josie Wentworth.

Wentworth. Cripes. Why couldn't she be a nosy Smith or Jones who was intent on finding his cousin Sabrina? But oh, no, not Josie. She had to be a Wentworth of the Wentworth Oil Works family.

Dandy, Max fumed. Just great. The rich got richer. In this case, they'd pad their coffers a bit more by suing him for Josie's accident and chalking up the Single C Ranch as one of their assets, albeit a meager one by their mighty standards.

No, damn it, he would *not* allow that to happen. He wasn't going to lose his ranch because the suit-and-tie lawyers belonging to the Wentworth clan stepped in to claim damages for Josie's knock on the head.

Get a plan, Carter, he told himself. Okay. What he needed was to sit Josie down and calmly and quietly explain that this spread was his life, his reason for being. To lose the Single C was to lose himself, who he was, his purpose for existing. Surely even a spoiled little rich girl, who wore designer jeans and had her nails professionally manicured could understand that.

But he couldn't have that heart-to-heart talk with Josie to ask her to call off the dogs in the form of her family attorneys, if she didn't remember who she was!

Max began to pace again, his mind going a hundred miles an hour. His glance fell on the sagging front steps.

He really ought to repair those, he thought absently, before they gave way under someone's weight and he was facing another lawsuit.

Josie. He quickly reminded himself of the troublesome subject at hand. She had clearly stated that her family had no clue that she'd been seeking him out. They didn't know where she was or how long she'd be away from Freemont Springs.

Excellent.

It was coming together in his mind like the pieces of a jigsaw puzzle. He would nurse Josie Wentworth back to memory-filled health himself, right here on the ranch. When she was as good as new, they'd have their sensible little chat, she'd go merrily on her way, and that would be that. Her family and the vulture lawyers need never know about Josie's accident. And time was on his side. Her family wasn't expecting her home anytime soon.

Lord, he was brilliant.

Max stopped pacing, nodded decisively, then frowned in the next instant.

There was one glitch in the genius-level plot, he realized. Josie had come to the Single C in search of Sabrina. Well, forget that. It was time Ms. Fancy Pants learned that people had a right to their privacy. Big bucks didn't always mean calling the shots and running roughshod over others' feelings.

Josie's quest to find Sabrina was self-centered and self-serving, and he wouldn't be a party to it. Whatever his cousin's involvement with Jack Wentworth had been, it was Sabrina's business, pure and simple. If she chose to contact the Wentworths, she would. If not, so be it.

There was also the fact that he had no idea where Sabrina was, Max thought dryly. He'd been very surprised to learn she'd given Jack Wentworth the Single C as an address to use to reach her by mail.

Maybe—hell, he didn't know what was going on—but maybe when Sabrina learned of Jack's death, she'd somehow known the Wentworths would be looking for her and had steered clear of the ranch because of it.

He was guessing, grabbing at straws, because what had actually transpired between Sabrina Jensen and Jack Wentworth was a complete mystery to him, as it was, apparently, to Josie.

Josie, Max thought again, dragging a restless hand

through his hair. Could he pull this off? Keep her here on the ranch until she was completely recovered? What if she demanded that he contact the family she couldn't remember so they could come and get her?

No way, he thought fiercely. He would *not* allow himself to be thrown to wolves in thousand-dollar suits. He'd have to lie, the idea of which was already causing a knot to tighten in his gut. But, damn it, his life, this ranch, was at stake.

Desperate situations called for desperate measures.

Max's tumbling-together thoughts were interrupted by Jeff's coming back out onto the porch. At the sound of the door, Max spun around.

"Well?" he said. "What's your verdict?"

Jeff walked forward slowly, rubbing one hand over his chin.

"Interesting," he said. "Textbook case. It's fascinating to be dealing with a situation that could have been lifted right out of a chapter I studied to pass an exam."

"Damn it, Jeff. Quit babbling and tell me what the deal is."

"Chill, Carter." Jeff paused. "Okay, here it is. Josie has a slight concussion. She needs to be wakened every hour until tomorrow morning to be certain she still knows how many fingers you're holding up, where she is—that type of thing."

"And?"

"And she has retrograde amnesia. At the moment she's a total blank, doesn't know who she is or why she's here. She's terribly frightened, by the way, so

I suggest you lighten up before you go back into the house.

"She could get her memory back in bits and pieces, or all at once. There's also a chance she might never remember a certain chunk of time. Say, for example, how she got the bump on the head."

"I should be so lucky," Max muttered.

"What?"

"Nothing. You have no idea how long this is going to last?"

"Nope."

"What a mess," Max said, shaking his head.

"Max, why is she here? She's a very beautiful woman. Is she at the Single C at your invitation? You know, your lady friend come to visit? What about her family? Are you going to contact them to let them know she's been injured?"

"Jeff, Jeff, Jeff," Max said, patting the doctor on the shoulder. "Don't concern yourself with the details. You did your job and I appreciate your coming out here. Send me a bill."

"You won't pay it."

"True. I'll trade you some prime beef for what I owe you."

"Sold. Well, I'm off. Give me a holler if you become concerned about Josie in any way. I called her Josie, but it didn't mean a thing to her. Man, I feel for her. She has a beaut of a headache and is scared spitless. It's got to be very frightening. I hope for her sake that this amnesia doesn't last long."

"Right," Max said, urging Jeff toward the steps of the porch.

"Maybe if she saw a member of her family, it would jog something loose," Jeff said, seemingly unaware that he was being propelled forward. "Do you know where—"

"Say hello to your lovely wife and kiddies for me," Max said.

"What? Oh, sure thing. I'll certainly do that. See ya, Max."

"Goodbye, Jeff. Thanks again."

Max stayed on the porch until Jeff had driven away and the dust had settled.

He was, Max knew, postponing going into the house and putting the lie into motion. He'd always prided himself on his integrity and honesty, the fact that his handshake and word were as good as gold.

But this situation with Josie had him cornered, fearful for his future, his land, everything he held dear. Little people with a little bit of money were powerless against the big boys with the big bucks.

In fairness to himself, Max reasoned, Josie had had no business coming to the Single C in the first place. She'd read a letter that was private and personal, not hers to open. She had choreographed a role for his cousin to play in regard to the Wentworth family—if, indeed, Sabrina had been seriously involved with brother Jack.

Josie had been way out of line.

She'd chosen a path, a course of action, she had no right to, and it had caused her nothing but grief—a bump on the head, a loss of her memory. Just desserts for a self-centered endeavor.

And he, Max Carter, was *not* going to pay the price for Josie Wentworth's selfish actions.

"All right," he said aloud, turning toward the door. "So be it."

In the living room Max walked to the sofa and stared down at Josie, his heart thundering instantly in his chest.

She was asleep, one hand curled loosely next to her pale cheek like a child. She looked vulnerable and delicate, causing him to fight against the urge to lift her gently into his arms and hold her, comfort her, assure her that everything was going to be fine.

No harm will come to you, Josie, he would tell her, *because I'm here, standing between you and anything that might threaten you.*

He frowned.

Lord, he thought, where was all that gooey, sentimental, macho junk coming from? He was no one's knight in shining armor. No way. He moved through life alone by choice and liked it just fine. He had even telegraphed that message by the name he'd given his ranch.

The women he dated and slept with on occasion understood his rules. No one got hurt. No commitments. No ties. No one telling him what to do or counting on him to be something he couldn't be.

Ms. Fancy Pants had gotten to him momentarily there because she was hurt, and Jeff had said she was scared to death. So, okay, he'd be patience personified, treat her kindly while she recovered.

Then they'd have their talk about how her accident

had been just that—an unfortunate mishap that was not fodder for a lawsuit.

After that? He'd send her packing back to her world of money and privilege, with *no* information whatsoever about Sabrina Jensen.

Josie moaned in her sleep, causing her lips to part slightly. Heated desire exploded in Max as he continued to gaze at her, envisioning his mouth claiming those inviting lips.

"Damn," he said, spinning on his heel and leaving the room.

He was still a grungy mess from the hard labor of dragging the tree stump out of the ground. He would take a shower and put on fresh clothes. He'd also hide Josie's car behind one of the outbuildings before it was time to waken her.

Yeah, he would go take a shower, and the water would be very, *very* cold.

She stirred and opened her eyes, one hand immediately lifting to her aching head. She'd slept deeply, felt foggy and disoriented, her mind a blur of confusion.

She blinked and waited for her eyes to focus properly, to bring into crystal clarity the details of a living room she recognized. She had obviously fallen asleep on a sofa, so...

The mist of sleep lifted and the chill of panic replaced it, causing her to whimper, the sound like that of a newborn kitten.

Dear heaven, she thought, it was coming back to her now. She'd been told by a kind doctor named

Jeff that she'd suffered a concussion from a fall. She was at a ranch called the Single C that was owned by a Max Carter.

Max. Yes. She'd seen him briefly before the doctor had arrived. Max Carter was very handsome, in an earthy, raw way, and very in need of a shower and clean clothes.

The doctor had explained that she had a case of amnesia due to her head injury. While definitely a frightening state to be in, it wasn't all that unusual under the circumstances. The best thing she could do to speed her recovery, he'd said, was to stay calm and to allow nature to take its course to restore her memory.

Stay calm?

She pressed trembling fingertips to her lips, willing herself not to cry.

"Josie," she whispered. "My name is Josie. The doctor called me that. Oh, God, why doesn't it mean anything to me? Josie? No. No. I don't know who that is. *I don't know who I am.*"

Max leaned against the kitchen wall out of view of the living room and curled his hands into tight fists.

Josie's tear-filled, softly spoken words had reached him, beating against him like physical blows.

He couldn't handle much of this, he thought. Josie *had* to get her memory back fast, because she was ripping him up. Big, tough Max Carter was being cut off at the knees by a sad, frightened and beautiful woman.

Get it together, Carter, he ordered himself. He would do what he had to do to survive this mess.

Oh, man, what he wouldn't give to turn back the clock to dawn of that morning. He'd headed out for hours of hard labor that would push his body to the maximum and beyond. At day's end he would have fallen into bed, exhausted and aching from head to toe. But he would have accomplished what he'd set out to do.

He would have had a weary but satisfying sense of accomplishment. But there would have been no one to share it with.

Max stiffened and planted his hands on his hips, a deep frown on his face.

Share it with? his mind echoed. Where had that harebrained thought come from? He didn't want anyone in his life to *share* with, for cripe's sake. He was alone by choice, damn it, not from lack of opportunity.

The unsettling events that had taken place today, the fact that Josie Wentworth was his to look after for heaven only knew how long, was scrambling his beleaguered brain.

He'd had enough of this. He'd really had enough. But that knot in his gut told him this nightmare was a long way from being over.

Hell.

Max strode into the living room and went directly to the sofa. Josie looked up at him questioningly, and he nearly groaned aloud as he saw the pallor of her cheeks, the stricken expression on her face, the fear in her huge eyes. He shifted his gaze to a spot just above her right shoulder.

"So!" he said, a tad too loudly. "I'm Max Carter, in case you've forgotten, and you're on my sofa." Lord, Carter, what a lame thing to say. "Anyway, there's nothing for you to worry about, because Jeff—he's the doctor who was here—said you're going to be fine. Soon. Very soon. Are you hungry?"

"I...I guess so," Josie said quietly. "Mr. Carter...Max...why did I come here to your ranch?"

"Don't strain your brain yet. Okay? The first order of business is to watch that concussion of yours until morning. I'll have to wake you every hour and ask you dumb questions. If you try to think too hard now, you'll only make your headache worse."

"Oh."

"Yeah, so I'll fix you some dinner and—"

"Where's my purse? Surely I had one. It would contain all kinds of identification, along with personal items that might jog my memory."

"Josie, you're pushing yourself. I just said you shouldn't do that."

"I know, but if I could examine the contents of my purse, I—"

"There is no purse. Nope. You had a suitcase, which I've put in the guest room. You...you arrived by taxi, you see, and maybe you left the purse in the cab by mistake."

Josie frowned. "A taxi? I wasn't driving my own car? Somehow that...just doesn't feel right."

"Nothing *feels* right, because you have a roaring

headache. How about some bacon and eggs? How do you like your eggs?"

"I don't know, but...yes, I like my bacon very crisp, nearly burned. Oh, Max, why do I know how I like bacon but not eggs?"

"Beats me," he said, shrugging. "Amnesia is weird stuff, isn't it? Yep. Sure is. Well, Josie, eggs and burned bacon coming right up."

Max hurried back into the kitchen, where he stopped dead in his tracks and took a deep, steadying breath.

No doubt about it, he thought gloomily, he wasn't going to survive this.

Josie watched Max's hasty exit from the room, studying the empty space long after he'd disappeared from view.

That man, she thought, was nervous and edgy, and seemed quite unable to meet her eyes. Why? Was he hiding something? Or was it simply that a woman with no memory perched on his sofa was throwing him off-kilter?

Oh, she didn't know. She didn't know *anything*. Well, that wasn't entirely true. One thing was clear. Max Carter was an extremely handsome man who just oozed sexuality. Had she come to the Single C at his invitation? For some type of liaison? Would she do something like that? If so, she certainly had good taste in men.

Oh, Josie, stop, she told herself. *You're getting hysterical.* Josie. That name still meant nothing to her, rang no bells. Josie. Was it short for Josephine?

That was rather old-fashioned. Had she been named after someone in her family?

She assumed she wasn't married, since she wore no wedding ring. But did she have parents? A sister? Brother?

A chill coursed through her.

Brother. There was something disturbing about the thought of a brother. But what? Damn it, what?

Oh, her head hurt.

Max was right. Straining her brain, as he'd so eloquently put it, was making the pain in her head unbearable. For now, at least, she'd put the subject of a brother on the back burner.

What she *should* be concentrating on was herself. Who was she? How old was she? Dear heaven, she didn't even know what she looked like.

Josie glanced quickly in the direction of the kitchen, where the sounds of pots and pans and slamming cupboard doors announced that Max was in the process of preparing her burned bacon.

Slowly, tentatively, she got to her feet, one hand pressed to her aching forehead. On unsteady legs she made her way across the room and down a narrow hallway. Finding a small bathroom, she hesitated, then lifted her chin and stepped in front of the mirror above a rust-stained sink.

A sob escaped her lips as she stared at her reflection.

She was looking at a stranger.

She had never seen the pale, stricken woman in the mirror before in her life.

Unable to move, hardly breathing, Josie watched two tears slide down the stranger's cheeks.

Chapter Five

Max set two plates of food on the table in the kitchen, then turned with the intention of going into the living room to tell Josie that dinner was ready. He stopped short when he saw her standing in the doorway.

"Oh," he said. "There you are. Well, such as it is, our meal is prepared."

Josie walked forward slowly. "Thank you. I hope you don't mind that I wandered through your home. I found my suitcase on a bed in a room down the hall and changed into a fresh blouse and..." She paused and sank onto a chair at the table. "I'm sorry. I'm babbling."

"Don't worry about it." Max settled onto the chair opposite her. "Eat as much as you can. You need to keep your strength up and, who knows, maybe some food in your stomach will make your headache ease a bit. I don't imagine you recall when you ate last."

"No." Josie spread the paper napkin in her lap. "Except—" she frowned "—doughnut holes. Cinnamon doughnut holes. I seem to remember eating... No, it's gone. It was just a flash, a picture of doughnut holes sort of floating through the air."

Max chuckled. "Too bad you can't grab a handful of them. You'll probably wish you had some after you taste my cooking."

Josie looked down at the offering on her plate. The bacon was, indeed, burned, but the scrambled eggs were a bit undercooked, the liquid beginning to edge its way around the plate.

"Try the toast," Max said, pushing a plate toward her. "I'm a culinary whiz at toast."

"I appreciate the effort you went to, Max. I feel like a nuisance, an intruder."

"Eat."

Josie picked up her fork and took a bit of eggs, forcing herself to chew and swallow. Max concentrated on consuming the food in front of him. Several minutes passed in total silence.

"Max," Josie said finally, "are you and I having an affair?"

Max had just taken a mouthful of coffee. He choked on it, coughing so hard he got to his feet and thumped himself on the chest.

"What kind of question is that?" he said when he could speak again.

"A perfectly reasonable one," Josie said, looking up at him. "You're an extremely handsome man, who obviously isn't married. I arrived with a suitcase, and you said I came in a taxi, which I apparently sent on its way, indicating I was planning to stay.

"The condition of my hands and nails, plus the expensive clothes I found in my suitcase suggest that I didn't come here to fill the position of a cleaning woman or housekeeper.

"So back to my question. Am I here to be with you? Are we having an affair?"

Max sank back onto his chair and glowered at Josie.

"Aren't you the little detective?" he said gruffly. "You have, I take it, reached the conclusion that you're wealthy."

Josie shrugged. "It would appear so, from the quality of my clothes and the genuine leather suitcase they're packed in."

"And since you tromped through my house, you realize I *don't* have money."

Josie matched Max's frown. "I haven't given it any thought. What is becoming very clear now, however, is that you have a giant chip on your shoulder about it."

"Let's just say that I wouldn't be having an affair with a woman of your financial standing. Okay?"

"That's a ridiculous reason not to become involved with someone," Josie said, her voice rising. "That's reverse snobbery."

"Whatever," he said, picking up his fork again. "Eat your dinner."

Josie leaned toward him. "You don't even like me, do you?"

"I don't even know you, lady!" Max yelled.

Oh, hell, he thought, he'd blown it. Josie had pushed, his temper had gotten in the way of his plan to keep his big mouth shut, and now she was staring at him with wide eyes.

She was no dope, this Ms. Josie Wentworth, and he could virtually see the questions getting ready to tumble, one after the next, from those kissable lips of hers.

"You don't know me?" Josie said incredulously. "Then why am I here with a suitcase, giving the distinct impression that I intend to stay?"

Be careful, Carter, Max warned himself. Maybe he could still pull this out of the fire. He had to tell Josie something, some little nibble to satisfy her for now. It had to sound halfway logical. *Think, Carter.* Or maybe he could lead Josie down another track altogether. Yeah, that was even better.

"I hope you realize how fortunate you are that I'm an honorable man," he said, narrowing his eyes. Honorable? Hell, he was turning into a bold-faced liar six ways to Sunday. "I could have answered that we were most definitely involved in an affair, then hustled you into bed as soon as you finished your lousy eggs."

Josie laughed. "Not a chance. I have a headache, remember?"

Heat coiled so suddenly, so tightly and so painfully in Max's belly at the sound of Josie's lilting laughter that his breath caught.

Look at her eyes, his mind thundered. Her big, fawn eyes were dancing, actually sparkling with merriment. Those lips, which were slowly, but surely, driving him insane with the desire to kiss them, were curved in a beautiful smile.

The last thing he'd expected was for her to laugh, to fill his shabby little room with a sound like wind chimes. His increased desire knocked him for a loop.

Josie patted her lips with the napkin and cleared her throat.

"I'm sorry," she said, unable to hide the last trace of her smile. "I couldn't resist." She paused. "Well, now I know that I have a sense of humor."

"That's a matter of opinion," Max said, glaring at her.

"And you *don't* have a sense of humor, Mr. Carter. You may be the sexiest man in these parts, but you're grumpy more often than not."

"I have a lot on my mind," he muttered.

Josie sighed. "I wish *I* did."

"Yeah, I know," he said quietly. "I realize that having amnesia must be frightening, Josie. You just have to relax, allow things to come back to you on their own. You're trying too hard, attempting to force it, and that obviously isn't going to work."

"We'll see. Will you at least tell me why I came to the Single C?"

Back to square one, Max thought. Okay, he'd give her a nibble, just a nibble. Easy does it.

"Okay, Josie," he said, "here it is. You got a bee in your bonnet to look up an old friend of yours, who happens to be my cousin. She mentioned me and this ranch at some point, so you started here. As for the taxi..."

He shrugged.

"You planned to telephone for another one when you were ready to leave, I guess," he went on. "You've already established the fact that you have plenty of money. You wouldn't think twice about having a cab drive all the way back out here to pick you up."

"I'm looking for your cousin?"

"Yep."

"What's her name?"

"Sabrina. She obviously isn't here, though. In fact, I haven't seen or heard from Sabrina in months."

"Sabrina," Josie said, sinking back in her chair. "That name doesn't ring any bells at all. She and I are old friends?"

Max nodded. "You go way back. Old school chums or something. You lost track of her, you were bored or whatever, and you decided to track her down. You of the rich jet set can do that kind of thing when the mood strikes, of course."

Josie smacked the table with the palm of one hand, causing her coffee to slosh over the rim of the mug.

"I've had quite enough of your nasty remarks regarding my economic status, Mr. Carter," she said. "I have no idea why you're so resentful of people in a higher tax bracket than you are, but *I* haven't done anything to offend you. The bottom line? Knock...it...off, mister."

Dynamite, Max thought. Josie Wentworth angry

was gorgeous beyond belief. Those incredible eyes of hers were now shooting laser beams at him, and her pale cheeks were flushed a pretty pink.

In the short time since she'd arrived to turn his life upside down, he'd seen her in so many different ways: sleeping like an innocent child, frightened and vulnerable, smiling and laughing, and now angry as a wet hen.

She was quite a package, all right, layer upon layer. She was obviously intelligent, too, as evidenced by some of the conclusions she'd drawn about herself.

Oh, yeah, Josie was really something. She also possessed the ability to cause heated desire to rocket through him at every turn.

Lord, how he wanted this woman.

He couldn't remember his body ever being so out of control. Josie was capable of pushing his buttons by doing nothing more than just being herself, just being here.

Well, forget it. He wasn't succumbing to the passion she evoked in him. He had no intention of becoming Josie's lover while she was at the Single C. He was a caregiver, nursing her back to health.

"Fine," he said. "I won't make any more remarks about your money or my lack of it."

"Thank you," Josie said, adding an indignant little sniff for good measure. "That's only fair, you know. Maybe I earned every dime I have.

"Let's see. My parents were poor, struggling to make ends meet, living paycheck to paycheck. I made up my mind early on that I wouldn't live my entire life that way. I worked hard and became a...an aeronautical engineer.'' She smiled. ''How's that?''

''Oh, okay,'' Max said, chuckling. ''That's very impressive.''

Josie's smile disappeared. ''Oh, Max, you have such a nice smile, you really do. You should use it more often.''

''I'll give it some thought.''

''Good.''

Their eyes met, held, and the room, the burned bacon and runny eggs, faded into oblivion. A strange mist seemed to swirl around them, encasing them in a cocoon that hummed with building, thrumming desire.

Max, Josie's mind whispered. Those eyes of his, those dark, compelling eyes, were pinning her in place, making it difficult to breathe.

Max. He was so big and strong, so powerful. What would it be like to be held in those beautifully muscled arms, then nestled against that rugged, massive body? He'd claim her lips, softly at first, then demanding more, which she'd give in total abandon.

Max. To make love with a man like him was beyond even *her* imagination. But...yes, he'd temper his strength with gentleness, put her pleasure before his own. He'd be an exquisite lover like none she'd ever experienced before. Somehow she just knew it.

Such heat. Dear heaven, the heat within her was like licking flames, consuming her with the want, the need, of Max Carter.

''Max?'' Josie said, her voice trembling.

''No,'' he said, pulling his gaze from hers.

"What's happening? What are you doing to me? You felt it, too. I know you did."

"Forget it, Josie," he said, getting to his feet. He planted his hands on the table and leaned toward her. "Yeah, okay, I felt it. I want you. I want to tear off your clothes and make love to you. Is that what you want to hear? Well, there, I've said it. But it isn't going to happen, not a chance."

"I—"

"No." Max straightened and sliced one hand through the air. "This discussion is over. We're healthy adults, who are extremely attracted to each other, but we're not going to do a damn thing about it. I am *not* going to make love with you, Josie."

"Well, who asked you to?" she said, glaring at him.

A very slow, very male smile crept onto Max's face and broadened into a grin that sent shivers slithering down Josie's spine.

"Darlin'," he said, "*you* did. It was there, loud and clear, in those fawn eyes of yours. Don't ever play poker, Josie, unless you wear mirrored sunglasses."

"Oh, you are so arrogant, so cocky, so—"

"Go for it. Think up a whole list of rotten adjectives that apply to me. It'll give you something to do until you get your memory back. I've got chores to tend to."

Max strode across the room and went out the back door.

"So full of yourself," Josie rattled on to the empty room. "So...so..." She sighed, plunked her elbow on the table and rested her chin on her palm. "So gorgeous it's sinful. Oh, Josie, get a grip."

Well, dandy, she thought. She'd just made a complete fool of herself, had come across like an adolescent panting after a movie star. Surely she didn't go around falling at men's feet all the time. No, she couldn't, wouldn't believe that of herself.

She knew—how, she wasn't certain—that she was acting out of character in regard to Max. He was dangerous, and he was drawing her down a path she didn't ordinarily travel. But her weakened, vulnerable condition was no excuse for her ridiculous, embarrassing behavior.

Well, she was now very aware of the effect Max had on her. She would stay on the alert, not fall prey to his masculine magnetism.

"So there," she said aloud.

She wrinkled her nose in the direction of the back door, then laughed softly at this final addition to her adolescent performance. In the next moment she glanced around the messy kitchen.

Her headache was much better. She should, she supposed, clean up, since Max had done the cooking. No problem. She could load a dishwasher as well as anyone.

Josie got to her feet, picked up the plates and walked toward the counter. She stopped, looked to the left, the right, then rolled her eyes heavenward.

Max Carter didn't *have* a dishwasher.

Max fully intended to stay busy in the barn until he was tired enough to drop and could be at least fairly certain Josie was asleep for the night.

"Oh, hell," he said aloud just after ten o'clock. He suddenly remembered that he was supposed to wake Josie every hour to assure that she was suffering no lingering effects from the concussion.

Wasn't that just great? He'd have to sit on the edge of her bed, call her name, maybe even touch her to waken her. He'd be in sexual agony, going up in flames. The night ahead was going to be the longest of his life.

Maybe Rusty... No, the old guy was sound asleep in his room at the end of the barn. The two other hands had their own places in town; they came out to the ranch at dawn and left at dusk.

There was no one to dump this on, Max thought, striding toward the house. Josie was *his* problem, pure and simple.

He was the one who was keeping her here with his lies in order to protect his land.

He was the one who'd decided Ms. Wentworth also needed to learn that people's private lives were just that—private.

So now *he'd* pay the piper. This was going to call for every bit of willpower he could muster.

In the kitchen he pulled off his boots, set his Stetson on the table and absently registered the fact that Josie had cleaned up after their meal.

He'd bet a buck, he thought crossly, she'd pitched a fit when she discovered he didn't have a dishwasher.

Good. She'd had to put her lily white hands and

manicured nails in a sinkful of hot, soapy water. That, Josie Wentworth, was how the other half lived.

Max sighed and sank onto one of the chairs at the table.

He was, he had to admit, coming on awfully strong about Josie's money and social status. He'd agreed that he would knock it off, and he would.

There was no one major incident that had created his dislike for the idle rich. It had simply been a lifetime of scraping out a living while observing those who had only to snap their fingers to get what they wanted.

He'd watched his father work himself into an early grave on a Texas ranch. His mother? She'd split when Max was two, having realized she was facing hard labor with few rewards for the endless years to come.

So, okay, he'd willingly chosen the same existence for himself when he'd bought the Single C, but by then his attitude about the rich getting undeservably richer was deeply entrenched in his mind.

Josie was one of *them,* and he wanted her off his land and out of his life as quickly as possible. He was *not,* however, running the risk of the Wentworth family's suing him for Josie's bump on the head.

A sudden thought struck him and he got to his feet, crossed the room and lifted the receiver from the wall telephone. A few minutes later he was speaking with Jeff Wilson.

"Get the drift?" Max said finally. "It just seems to me that Josie is better off getting a solid night's sleep than having me disturb her every hour."

"Well, any medical textbook would say she should be wakened every hour to be certain she still knows basic information, that sort of thing."

"Forget the books, Jeff. She ate dinner, cleaned the kitchen, carried on a lengthy conversation with me during the meal."

Max, are you and I having an affair?

"Believe me," Max said dryly, "her busy little mind was going nonstop."

"Is she asleep now?"

"I assume so. I just got in from the barn."

"Okay, we'll compromise," Jeff said. "Go wake her, ask her some questions, the whole nine yards. If she's got it together after having been asleep, then don't wake her again. But, Max, if she suffers increased pain in her head, double vision or dizziness tomorrow, call me right away."

"Fine. Thanks, Jeff."

"You must be getting old, Carter."

"Why?"

"You're talking a blue streak to stay *out* of a beautiful woman's bedroom. Yep, you hit thirty on your last birthday and you're losing it."

"Good night, Jeff."

Max hung up the receiver with the sound of Jeff's laughter echoing in his ear.

He decided he was hungry, and he made and consumed a sandwich he really didn't want. His next conclusion was that the gentlemanly thing to do was to take a shower before waking Josie, instead of having her assaulted by the odors of sweat and horse manure.

Finally, clad only in a clean pair of jeans, Max realized he was completely out of ideas on how to postpone the inevitable, other than washing the living room walls or vacuuming the floor, neither of which appealed.

He walked slowly, very slowly, from his bedroom to the one he'd designated the guest room, then stopped in the open doorway.

The curtain on one of the windows didn't close properly and bright moonlight was pouring over the bed like a silvery waterfall. Heart thundering, Max moved next to the bed and stared down at Josie.

Her auburn hair was fanned out on the pillow, the moonlight making it appear like strands of polished copper. Her skin looked like lush velvet, causing his fingertips to tingle with the urge to stroke her soft cheek, then sift through her hair.

Heat churned in him, a hot, tight, aching.

A moonlight angel, his mind whispered. That was what Josie was, lying there so still, as though sculpted from the finest ivory. She was the picture of feminine beauty, woman to his man.

Max started to sit down, hesitated, drew a steadying breath, then settled carefully on the bed next to Josie's slender hip. The blanket was drawn to just below her breasts, which were covered by a pale pink T-shirt. He jerked his gaze from her breasts to concentrate on her face.

''Josie,'' he said, hardly recognizing the gritty quality of his voice. ''Josie, wake up.''

She didn't move.

''Josie,'' he repeated more loudly.

Max closed his eyes for a moment and shook his head.

He was going to have to touch her, he realized, opening his eyes again and becoming aware of his feelings of panic. He'd... Okay, he'd jiggle her shoulder. That was safe enough. A shoulder that was just inches from her breast. No, forget the shoulder.

He'd tap gently on her cheek...but that was next to those kissable lips that were driving him right out of his ever-lovin' mind.

For cripe's sake, Carter, he admonished himself. Just pick a spot and do it. Wake Josie up, ask her something inane—like what she'd had for dinner—then get the hell out of the room.

Do it, Carter. Now.

In Josie's dream she was snuggled in a bed that had been placed in a field of wildflowers. Somehow she knew she mustn't move until Max came, until Max touched her, caressed her, made it clear that at last, *at last,* he was going to gather her into his strong arms, hold her and kiss her.

Make love with her.

She was waiting for Max.

And she wanted him so very, very much.

With a hand that was not quite steady, Max nestled his palm on Josie's cheek.

"Josie," he said, "it's me, Max. Wake up. Josie?"

Josie's lashes fluttered, then she opened her eyes, a lovely smile forming instantly on her lips.

"Max," she whispered, "you came, just as I knew you would."

Max snatched his hand from her cheek.

"What?" he said, frowning.

"I was waiting for you and now you're here." Josie's arms floated upward, reaching toward him. "Oh, Max."

She sat up and leaned forward, entwining her arms around his neck. He stiffened and swallowed heavily.

"Max?" Josie said, a catch in her voice. "What is it? What's wrong? Don't you want to hold me, touch me, kiss me? Don't you want to make love with me, Max?"

And Max Carter was lost.

With a groan that rumbled deep in his chest, he wrapped his arms around Josie, then lowered his head and claimed her lips in a searing kiss.

Chapter Six

The kiss was fire.

The embers of desire that had smoldered within Josie and Max from the moment they'd met burst into raging flames that consumed their bodies and overrode their ability to think, to reason, to remain linked to the reality of the wrong or right of what they were doing.

There was only the kiss. And the fire. And the burning want and need.

Max lifted his head a fraction of an inch, then slanted his mouth in the other direction, capturing Josie's lips once more, delving with his tongue into the sweet moist darkness of her mouth.

He drank of her taste, inhaled her aroma of fresh air and flowers, savored the feel of her delicate body encased in his arms.

Josie returned the urgent, hungry kiss with a hunger of her own, inching her fingertips into Max's thick hair, urging his mouth even harder onto hers. She didn't think, she only felt, giving way to her passion.

Max was so powerful, so strong, and his embrace made her feel feminine and protected. He smelled so good, like soap and man. His bare skin was taut and smooth, the play of muscles beneath her roving hands heightening her desire.

At last she broke the kiss to speak close to Max's lips.

"Oh, Max, please," she whispered. "I need you. I want you so very much."

Max didn't speak. He got to his feet to shed his jeans, then threw back the blankets and drew Josie's T-shirt up, tossing it onto the floor.

He gazed at her naked form for a long, heart-stopping moment, the moonlight cascading over her.

Moonlight angel, his hazy mind hammered. *His* moonlight angel. Josie was exquisite. She was the essence of what had been missing from his life. She filled a void to overflowing, an emptiness he hadn't even known existed.

But now she was here. Josie.

He lifted her and moved her into the center of the bed, following her down, seeking, then finding her mouth again. He splayed one hand on her flat stomach, relishing the feel of her dewy skin beneath his callused palm.

He shifted from her lips to one breast, drawing the

sweet, sweet bounty into his mouth, laving the nipple to a taut bud with his tongue.

Josie murmured in pure feminine pleasure.

Max paid homage to her other breast as he rested his weight on his forearm, his free hand skimming along the gentle slope of Josie's hip, then down her slender leg.

Fire.

It was too much to bear, had to be quelled before the licking flames devoured them, turning them into ashes to be scattered by the wind.

"Max," Josie said, her voice a near sob.

He moved over her, then into her, thrusting deep, filling her. Then he stilled, drinking in the sight of her in the moonlight, memorizing all he saw.

Josie smiled. It was a womanly smile, so soft, so gentle. It was a smile of wisdom, of acceptance, of joy that she was his counterpart.

"Max."

That was all she said, just his name, in a voice hushed and reverent.

A strange, aching sensation gripped Max's throat as the sound of his own name flowed over him with a soothing warmth.

He didn't speak. He *couldn't* speak. He began to move within Josie's body, slowly at first, then increasing the tempo, his gaze never leaving hers.

Harder. Faster. Thundering.

Josie matched him beat for beat.

They were one entity, meshed, perfect.

They soared toward the summit of their exquisite journey, higher, reaching...reaching...needing...

"Max!"

He flung back his head as he found his release a second after Josie was hurled into oblivion. They clung to each other tightly, shuddering as wave after wave of ecstasy swept through them.

Max collapsed against Josie, spent, sated. He rolled to his side, taking her with him, then leaving her body so very reluctantly. He pulled the sheet over their slick, cooling bodies, then nestled Josie's head on his shoulder. Breathing quieted. Hearts returned to normal rhythms.

"Max," Josie said.

"Shh," he said. "Don't."

Josie nodded her agreement not to speak, then her lashes drifted down and she sighed in contentment just before giving way to the somnolence that claimed her.

Max stared into space as again and again he sifted his fingers through Josie's silken hair. Stark reality returned like a painful, physical blow, and a knot tightened in his gut.

Damn it, he thought furiously, he'd lost control, had succumbed to his burning desire for Josie, with no regard for the consequences.

He'd had sex... Ah, hell, who was he kidding? He'd *made love* with a woman who didn't even know who she was or what her values were. He'd taken advantage of her, taken all she'd offered him, not caring that it was wrong, so damn wrong.

And the emotions that had consumed him while making love with her were unsettling, nearly terrifying. He'd felt so complete, so whole. He could remember thinking that so much had been missing from his life before that moment. Before Josie.

No, damn it, it wasn't true. He didn't need Josie. He didn't need anyone. He had his ranch, the lifestyle he wanted, and he was completely satisfied with his existence as it stood.

Then why had he registered those emotions? Why had... No, forget it. Forget everything that had happened in this room, in this bed, he told himself.

He shifted his weight, slid his arm carefully from beneath Josie's head so as not to waken her, then eased off the bed. He grabbed his jeans from the floor and strode from the room, forcing himself not to look back to where Josie slept in the glow of the moonlight.

Fingers of sunlight tiptoed across Josie's face, nudging her awake. As the fogginess of sleep lifted, she was gratefully aware of the fact that she did *not* have a headache.

She stretched like a lazy kitten, then stilled as she felt the slight soreness in her body that was accompanied by vivid, sensual images of making love with Max.

Dear heaven, she thought, sitting bolt upward in the bed. What had she done?

The sheet slid to her waist, revealing her bare breasts, and she grabbed the material, clutching it with both hands beneath her chin.

Oh, where was the amnesia when she needed it? she thought frantically. She did not want to remember that *she* had been the aggressor, the seducer, the previous night.

Max had wakened her, as per the doctor's instructions, to make certain she was still lucid after her nasty bump on the head.

Lucid? As in sane? Not hardly. She'd been dreaming about Max, then Max had been there, sitting on the edge of the bed.

Then she'd—

"Oh-h-h," she moaned, sinking back on the pillow.

She'd flung herself at Max Carter, literally begged him to make love with her. He was a lusty, healthy man, who hadn't stood a chance against her wanton behavior. She'd taken advantage of him, pure and simple.

She was so mortified she wanted to die.

She, Josie Whoever-she-was, *should* be mortified. She was truly ashamed of herself.

Never mind that making love with Max had been so incredibly beautiful it defied description. She had no recollection of previous lovers, but instinct told her that what she'd shared with Max had been far more exquisite than anything she'd experienced before.

It hadn't been just sex. No, it had been making love, with precious emotions of caring, wishing to give pleasure to Max, feeling so protected, feminine, special, in his embrace. They had been perfect together, like two pieces of an intricate puzzle.

Soul mates.

"Oh, Josie, stop it," she said aloud. "Slow down. Get a grip."

Max Carter was *not* her soul mate. He was *not* the man she'd been destined to meet, to marry, to spend her life with. Heavenly days, that was absurd. For all she knew, she had a string of lovers waiting for her wherever it was that she lived.

If she wanted to marry and have a family, wouldn't she have done so by now? She was attractive, intelligent, had a sense of humor. Had she chosen to remain single because she liked the social life, the jet-set scene, the bed-hopping?

No. That didn't feel right, didn't fit, like a pair of shoes that weren't hers. No. She wasn't promiscuous.

Then why, why, why had she been so determined to make love with Max? Why was a section of her beleaguered brain savoring the knowledge that she'd done exactly that? How could she explain to herself that a part of her wasn't sorry about what had happened—was, in fact, glorying in the memory of every sensuous detail?

Oh, she didn't know. She was so confused, so muddled. It was difficult enough having no memory beyond waking up with a roaring headache on Max's sofa. Now she'd complicated her life further by making love with a man she hardly knew.

Wondrous love.

Exquisite love.

The mere thought of their lovemaking caused desire to once again thrum through her body with a heat that threatened to consume her.

"Enough," Josie said, flinging back the sheet and leaving the bed.

She'd shower and dress, then find some lifesaving coffee. And somewhere in the midst of those mundane activities, she hoped she'd figure out how she was going to face the man she had wantonly seduced.

When Max was nowhere to be found in the house, Josie realized she was not that surprised. Ranchers were up and at it at dawn.

Would Max come in for lunch? she wondered. How many hours did she have to get through before the dreaded confrontation?

After consuming two cups of coffee and a slice of toast, she cleaned the kitchen, then wandered aimlessly around the small living room.

What did she usually do all day? Did she have a demanding career? Was she wealthy to the point that she did only volunteer work? Just how much money did she have, and where had it come from?

She didn't know, but at the moment she was definitely bored, couldn't spend another second wearing out Max's already threadbare carpet.

She left the house and headed for the barn.

If Max was in the big, red building, so be it. She had to look him in the eye at some point today. She just wished she had a clue about what she was going to say to him.

In the barn Josie called out a cheerful hello, which was answered with total silence.

"Great," she muttered. "Nobody's home, not even the weird horse."

She stopped in her tracks and frowned.

Weird horse? What weird... Wait! Yes, there had been a strange animal and a wagon and an old cowboy named Dusty... No, no, his name...his name was Rusty.

Josie closed her eyes, strained her mind, struggling for more details.

She was standing by the wagon, contemplating how to get up onto the wooden seat so that Rusty could take her to where Max Carter was. She'd shifted her purse strap higher onto her shoulder and finally managed to climb—

Josie's eyes flew open.

Her purse?

A wave of dizziness swept over her and she stumbled forward to sink onto a bale of hay next to a wall. Leaning her head back against the rough wood, she drew a steadying breath, then sighed with relief when the barn quit spinning around her.

She had *not,* she knew, left her purse in the taxi as Max had suggested. She couldn't at this point remember anything beyond settling next to Rusty on the high seat, but she definitely knew she'd had her purse with her on that wagon.

So, that meant...what? She'd dropped her purse someplace between here and where Rusty had taken her? That didn't seem feasible if there'd been a long strap attached to the purse she'd secured on her shoulder.

A chill coursed through her and she wrapped her hands around her elbows.

Had Max Carter lied to her? Somewhere on this

ranch was there a purse that held the answers to who she was and where she lived?

She shook her head. That didn't make sense. Why would Max wish to hide her identity from her? If she knew who she was and she had a family, they could come to the Single C and pick her up, get her out of Max's way.

What purpose would it serve Max to intentionally keep her on his ranch?

"Oh, my gosh, I've been kidnapped," she said, jumping to her feet.

In the next moment she sank back on the hay, clicking her tongue in self-disgust.

That was ridiculous. If Max was a kidnapper, he wasn't very good at it. He'd gone blissfully off to do whatever ranchers did all day, leaving her with full access to a telephone.

If she chose to do so, she could call the police, explain her dilemma and ask if there was a missing-person report on someone matching her description.

Yes, she could certainly do that.

And she knew, as quickly as the idea had come to her, that she didn't intend to pursue it. She was going to stay right here on the Single C until her memory was restored.

She was going to stay right here...with Max.

"Oh, Josie," she whispered. "You're being so foolish."

But she didn't care. She felt as though she'd been transported to another planet, where she didn't know who she was, nor where she'd come from. It was a magical place that was hers to enjoy, savor, reaping its rewards until it was time to leave.

And on that planet was the most magnificent man imaginable. Max.

So foolish, she repeated mentally. She should be in a state of constant panic over her lack of memory, be so frightened she was nearly hysterical.

Instead, she was viewing the situation as an adventure, a gift, a chance to do and be whatever felt right at any given moment.

Her memory was already beginning to return in bits and pieces. She didn't doubt for a second that there would be no permanent damage from her silly bump on the head. She'd go back to her own world very soon.

In the meantime there was Max.

"You're a wanton hussy, Josie," she said aloud, smiling brightly. "Shame on you."

But then her smile faded and turned into a frown.

She must be very, very careful. She was giving herself this time on the Single C as a present to be cherished, the memories of it hers to keep. But when she left here, she must be certain that she didn't leave her heart behind.

She must *not* fall in love with Max Carter.

"Fine," she announced, getting to her feet. "No problem. I've got this all figured out."

Except for one niggling little item, she thought, walking out of the barn. What had happened to her purse?

Josie wandered back to the house and entered through the rear door. She gasped, her heart racing with sudden fright as she came face-to-face with a woman who was standing in the kitchen. A very pregnant woman.

"Oh, I'm so sorry if I startled you," the woman said. "You must be Josie. I'm Sally Wilson, Jeff's wife. He was the doctor who tended to your head injury. Do you remember him?"

"Yes, of course," Josie said, smiling. "He's a very nice man."

"I think so, too," Sally said, matching Josie's smile.

Josie's gaze shifted to Sally's stomach.

"A baby," Josie said softly. "How wonderful. I want to have a baby." She blinked, then felt a flush of heat stain her cheeks. "Where did that come from?"

Sally shrugged. "Your subconscious, I guess. I don't know anything about amnesia, but it must be how you feel because you said it. You want to have a baby. That's a perfectly reasonable desire."

"I suppose it is, but the idea doesn't seem the least bit familiar to me. I wonder if that's because I've never acknowledged it before.... Well, never mind. Are you looking for Max?"

"No. Heaven knows where he is," Sally said. "He leaves his door unlocked and I come by on my egg-delivery day and put a dozen in his refrigerator."

"Oh, I see," Josie said, nodding.

Sally laughed. "My mother watches the kids on egg day. That's my big outing of the week. I get to visit with people on my route. I rarely see Max, though."

"You have other children?" Josie said.

Sally patted her stomach. "This is number four."

Josie narrowed her eyes. "I'm waiting to see if I get a flash on how many babies I want." She paused. "Nope. No messages coming in."

"You're awfully calm about having lost your memory," Sally said. "Jeff said you were very frightened, but it doesn't appear to me that you are."

"Oh, believe me, I was, but I'm beginning to remember little things. I'm sure I'll be completely recovered very soon. I decided not to get stressed out in the meantime."

"Good for you. Except..." Sally frowned.

"Except what?"

"What if you have a family, people who are frantic with worry because you didn't return on time?"

"I've thought about that," Josie replied. "Max said I came here to find an old school chum who happens to be his cousin. It seems to me that I wouldn't know how long it would take to find her and so probably told any family I might have that I didn't know when I'd be back."

"That makes sense," Sally said. "Well, super. You can just sit back and enjoy Max Carter's company. Maybe you can get him to smile every now and then. He's a good friend, but he's very... Oh, how should I put it? Max is closed, guarded, solitary. He gives the impression that he's a loner who doesn't need anyone close to him. I don't believe it for a second."

"You don't?" Josie raised her eyebrows.

"No, not when Jeff and I see him with our kids.

They adore their uncle Max and he's so patient with them. He plays games, reads them stories, takes them for walks, all kinds of things."

"He does?"

"Yes, indeed, and Max actually smiles *a lot* when he's with the children. He should have a family of his own. In my opinion, Josie, the Single C is the wrong name for this spread."

"Fascinating," Josie said.

Sally laughed. "I have noticed, however, that Max doesn't ask for my opinion." She glanced at her watch. "Oh, my, look at the time. I've got to dash. It was lovely talking to you. I'll report to Jeff that you're coming along just fine. Bye for now."

"Goodbye, Sally," Josie said, smiling. "It was a pleasure to meet you."

When Sally left and silence settled over the room again, Josie sat down at the kitchen table, mulling over everything the doctor's wife had said.

"Interesting," she said finally. "Very interesting."

There were obviously many layers to Max Carter. He was a mystery waiting to be unraveled.

Which Max would return to the house at the end of his long day of labor?

The grumpy, scowling Max?

The one with heated desire radiating from his compelling dark eyes?

A smiling, laughing man, such as Sally Wilson had described?

Josie didn't know, but she was definitely going to be here to find out.

* * *

The first vibrant colors of sunset were beginning to streak across the sky when Max finished tending to his horse, then left the barn for the house.

He was bone-weary and starving to death. He'd worked straight through the day, not returning to the house for lunch—because he hadn't yet been prepared to face Josie.

He'd fumed at himself the entire day for having made love to her. He'd lost control and taken advantage of a woman who was vulnerable. He was a rat.

Had Josie spent the day crying over what had happened last night? Lord, that was a depressing thought. Or maybe she'd worked herself up into a fury that would earn him a pop in the chops when he walked through the door. Fine. He deserved that and worse.

He had to apologize, make it up to Josie somehow. The only thing he had to give her—besides a spoken token of remorse—was her identity. So be it. He'd tell her she was Josie Wentworth of Wentworth Oil Works and let the lawsuit chips fall where they may.

Damn, what a mess, but he had no one to blame but himself.

He stopped outside the back door of the house, removed his Stetson, took a deep breath and entered the kitchen.

Josie was standing in front of the stove. She turned at the sound of the door closing.

"Hi, Max," she said, smiling brightly. "You're supposed to say, 'Honey, I'm home,' like they do in the movies.

"Guess what? I'm beginning to get my memory back. I'm remembering little bits and pieces. Isn't that great?

"Oh, and I discovered two important things about myself today.

"One, I can't cook, so there are frozen dinners in the oven."

"And two?"

"I want to have a baby."

Chapter Seven

Max opened his mouth to speak, closed it again, then shook his head slightly.

"What?" he finally managed to say.

Josie frowned. "Do you want me to repeat all that?"

"No, no." Max raised one hand. "I'm digesting it...slowly."

"Well, good. This gourmet meal won't be ready for about forty-five minutes if you want to shower or whatever."

"You're, um, certainly in a chipper mood," Max said, eyeing her warily.

Josie shrugged. "Yes, I guess I am. And you?"

"My frame of mind is not the issue here. Could we back up to the part about the baby?"

"Oh, that. Well, you see, Sally Wilson was here

delivering your eggs. She's a delightful person, really lovely. Anyway, when I saw her obviously pregnant state, I realized that I wanted to have a baby, too. I'm not certain, of course, but I believe that I didn't know that about myself before now."

"A baby." Max dragged one hand down his face. "Josie, we made love last night."

"I'm aware of that, Max. I was there."

"Yes, well, are you protected? Using some kind of birth control?"

"Oh." Josie's eyes widened. "I...I have no idea. I really don't know."

"Hell." Max stared at the ceiling for a long moment, then glared at her. "That's just great."

"Wait a minute. I don't recall you worrying about it at the time. It's as much your responsibility as mine, mister."

Max sighed and shook his head in self-disgust. "You're right. I'm sorry I barked at you."

"Max," Josie said quietly, "we need to talk about what happened last night."

"Yeah, I know," he said wearily. "Let me go shower and change. My clothes are so dirty and sweaty they could stand up on their own. I won't be long."

Well, this was it, Josie thought, as Max left the room. When Max returned to the kitchen, she was going to have to apologize for her behavior of the previous night. And Max Carter was *not* in a sunshine mood.

Max stood under the stinging spray of the shower, lathering his body with soap.

Well, he thought, this was it. When he walked back into that kitchen, he could no longer postpone the apology he owed Josie for taking advantage of her the night before.

Josie's upbeat frame of mind was about to be blown to smithereens by the reality-check discussion they were going to have.

As he sluiced the soap away, he thought about her. It had been strange, very different, to come in off the range to find a woman in his kitchen preparing dinner, such as it was.

A smiling woman.

An I'm-really-glad-you're-home-Max woman.

More precisely a woman named Josie Wentworth.

Who wanted to have a baby.

"Good Lord," Max said, then sputtered and coughed as he swallowed a mouthful of water.

A baby, his mind kept echoing. He dried off, then dressed in jeans and a navy blue sweatshirt. A baby.

Josie with a child suckling at her breast.

His child.

Josie's laughter ringing through this old house like wind chimes, accompanied by children's giggles.

His children.

His and Josie's.

"Can it, Carter," he muttered as he sat on the edge of his bed to put on sweat socks.

He was thinking like a crazy man. It was amazing what damage the lack of food could do to a person's brain.

He did *not* want a wife and baby.

His life was simple and orderly. He got up, worked himself into a state of exhaustion, then went to bed.

Max stared into space.

That was it? The sum total of his existence? Well, yeah, he guessed it was, but he liked it that way. Right? Right. Each day was a repeat of the one before, varied only by the chores that needed tending to. Fine. That was just fine.

Why was he wasting his mental energy justifying his life-style? Yes, of course, he knew why. He was once again postponing facing Josie, and all that he needed to say to her.

"Enough," he said, getting to his feet.

Max left the bedroom and strode down the hall, a deep frown on his face.

Josie was sitting at the table when he came into the kitchen, her state of nerves finally resulting in trembling legs that had refused to support her for another second. Her hands were clutched tightly in her lap as Max settled in the chair opposite her.

Oh, wasn't this cute? she thought. They were dressed alike in dark blue sweatshirts and jeans. Yep, just cute as a button. And she was getting hysterical, she knew she was. She had to get a grip.

"Max—"

"Josie—"

They'd spoken at the same time, then stopped.

"Go ahead," Max said.

"Oh, no, I'll wait," Josie said quickly.

Max dragged one hand through his damp hair, leaving tracks where his fingers had been.

"Last night," he began, "was... First of all, Josie, it was wonderful, the lovemaking we shared. I want to go on record as having said that."

"Oh, yes, Max, it truly was."

"The thing is...Josie, it shouldn't have happened and I feel..."

"I know, I know," she said miserably. "You feel taken advantage of, and I realize that my behavior was despicable and it wasn't your fault, because I was so...so wanton and aggressive, and I'm so very sorry, but then again I'm not, because it was so beautiful and rare and special and..." Josie halted and drew a much-needed gulp of air.

"Huh?" Max said, leaning toward her.

"Max Carter," Josie said, nearly shrieking, "didn't you hear one word of what I just said?"

"Yes, of course, I did, but...Josie, I was going to apologize for taking advantage of *you.*"

"Huh?"

"This is nuts," he said, sinking back in his chair.

"No joke." She frowned. "Now what do we do?"

"Well, I guess we agree that we made love by mutual consent."

"We do? We did?"

Max shrugged. "That's easier to deal with than figuring out who should be apologizing to whom."

"You've got a point there." Josie raised one finger in the air.

"Good, that's settled, then. We should have discussed this before I left the house this morning. I've put in one helluva long day beating myself up about it."

"So have I." Josie paused. "Max?"

"Hmm?"

"What about tonight?"

"Tonight?" he said, raising one eyebrow.

Josie got to her feet and began to pace the floor in front of the table.

"Unless you want me to leave the Single C," she began, "turn myself over to the police as a missing person in reverse or whatever, I'd like to stay here until my memory returns."

Max's gaze was riveted on Josie as she went from one end of the table to the other.

"As I told Sally Wilson," she continued, "I don't think my family, if I have one, is frantic about where I am. If I set out to find an old school chum, I must have told my parents or whoever that I didn't know how long I'd be gone."

"You said something to me along those lines," Max said, nodding.

"Yes, well, I don't believe it'll be a great deal of time before I remember everything, because I'm already getting flashes of this and that. So, I'm treating this like...oh, I don't know, like a slice of hours, days, that are mine to do with as I choose."

"I see."

"I have no idea what type of responsibilities I might have back where I live, but for now I'm just me, Josie, with no last name."

Wentworth, Max's mind yelled. She was Josie Wentworth of Wentworth Oil Works. He was going to tell her that right now. He couldn't live with his duplicity any longer.

But…

If he divulged her identity, Josie would be gone, probably within the hour. He'd never see her again. He'd get to know the Wentworth attorneys all too soon, but Josie would be removed from his life forever.

Damn it, no. Not yet.

Josie stopped her trek and looked directly at him. "May I stay here on your ranch until my memory is restored, Max?"

"Yes."

"Then we're back to the question—what about tonight and tomorrow night and… We're consenting adults. We need to have a mature, calm discussion about…about…" Josie's voice trailed off and she frowned.

"About?" Max prompted.

Josie stomped back to her chair and sat down, folding her arms across her breasts and scowling.

"Something tells me I've never done anything like this before," she said. "I'd appreciate it if you'd help me out a bit here."

"Oh, sure thing." Max cleared his throat. "We're discussing—maturely and calmly—whether or not we're going to sleep together for the duration of your stay at the Single C."

"Exactly," Josie said, smiling brightly. "Do we or do we not want to have an affair while I'm here? No strings attached. No commitments. When I'm fully recovered, I'll just ride off into the sunset."

Max frowned. "That sounds a tad cold."

"No, it isn't," she said, flinging out her arms.

"Not if that's what we agree to. Neither of us can possibly get hurt if we understand the rules.

"We're extremely attracted to each other and we seem to care about each other. We would make love, Max, create beautiful memories, then I'd leave and that would be that."

"We'd never see each other again," he said quietly.

A sudden chill swept through Josie as though a dark cloud had appeared and was hovering over her.

"No," she said, her voice a near whisper. "We'd never see each other again."

Fine, Max thought. That was fine. Hey, he knew guys who would kill for a situation like this one. For a stretch of time he could have a gorgeous, sensuous, delectable woman in his bed every night, with no worries about her making demands on him or getting fanciful ideas about snaring him into marriage and babies.

So why was he hesitating? Why wasn't he shouting, "You betcha, babe!" then concentrating on getting some food into his empty stomach?

We'd never see each other again.

Those words, which seemed to hang in the air like shadows of gloom, were unsettling him. That was because he'd never done anything like this before, he told himself.

He could handle this. He'd be a fool not to agree to the plan. He didn't want a wife and babies. Josie was willing to be his lover with no plan to rope him into anything more.

It just didn't get better than this.

So? *Go for it, Carter.*

"Okay, Josie," he said. "I see no problem. We'll be lovers while you're here at the Single C. No strings. No commitments. Oh, and I'll take care of the birth control, since you don't know if you're protected. When your memory is restored, you'll leave. I understand and accept those rules." Max paused. "Could I add one little item?"

"Certainly."

"Our dinner is burning."

Late that night Josie lay next to Max in his bed, absently twining her fingers in the moist, dark curls on his chest.

They'd made beautiful, exquisite love that had left them sated and inching toward sleep.

"Max?" Josie said.

"Hmm?"

"When I leave here, I guess I'll continue to search for your cousin, Sabrina. I will have remembered why she and I were such close friends, what made me decide to seek her out. Do you have any idea where she is?"

Max frowned into the darkness. "Josie, did it ever occur to you that if Sabrina wanted to keep in touch with you, she would have done so?"

"Well, people lose track of each other, even close friends. I want—"

"There's the clincher," he interrupted. "*You* want. You were bored or whatever, and you decided to find Sabrina. Maybe she doesn't want you to find her."

"What are you getting so grumpy about?" Josie asked, flattening her hand on his chest.

"I just think that people have a right to their privacy, that's all. I certainly don't like *my* privacy invaded."

"Oh, is that so?" Josie wriggled out of Max's embrace and sat up, covering her bare breasts with the sheet.

"You mean that if we were just talking, attempting to get to know each other better, and I asked you why you're so dead set against getting married, you'd refuse to answer me?"

"Got it in one."

"And your crummy attitude about people with money? You'd pass on commenting on that subject, too?"

"Yep."

"Why? That doesn't make sense."

"Neither topic is a deep, dark secret of mine, Josie. It's the principle of the thing. You're talking about my *private* beliefs and opinions. They are, quite frankly, none of your business." And to be honest, he was scared to let her get too close to him, to his heart, his soul.

"Well!" she said indignantly. "So much for sharing."

"There's a fine line between sharing and being plain old nosy."

"But—"

"Come here," he said, wrapping one arm around her waist. "Let's quit gabbing and indulge in the kind of sharing you and I do best.'' He pulled her down and rolled her on top of him. ''Agreed?''

''For now,'' Josie said, as heated desire shimmered through her.

''Good. You're good. We're good...together.''

Josie laughed. ''That's a whole bunch of good.''

''You betcha, babe.''

Then no more words were spoken.

The following two weeks flew by so quickly it was as though a magical wind was whipping the pages of the calendar, one after the other.

Josie and Max began their day early, sharing breakfast duties. Josie burned the bacon. Max produced runny scrambled eggs and perfect toast.

Then Max set out to tackle the chores of the day, while Josie, to her own fascination, spent her time thoroughly enjoying weeding, trimming and generally sprucing up the front yard.

She had no real interest in housework, she discovered, but once outside she had to be called more than once by Max to come into the house for lunch. She filed down her nails and dug her hands deep into the soil, removing the unwanted intruders and revealing lush, green grass.

The nights were heavenly, full of passion never fully quelled, leaving embers of desire that were ignited once again with a look, a touch, a smile.

Each day brought new flashes of memory to Josie. She now knew that her favorite color was blue.

She lived somewhere high above the ground in a place that was cool, peaceful and inviting, dominated by somewhat confusing images of fluffy, white clouds.

She saw the rich leather of the binding on rows of books, but couldn't decipher where they were actually located, often getting the impression they were in two different areas.

There had been one image in her mind of a weeping little girl wearing saddle shoes, knee socks and some type of uniform. She'd been surrounded by two boys and a man, whose faces she couldn't see clearly. The taller boy had leaned toward the child she assumed was her, then the tears had stopped and a smile materialized.

Did she have a brother? Josie wondered. Two brothers? Was the man her father? Where was her mother?

Whenever her mind skittered to the thought of a brother, a feeling of foreboding swept through her. She mentally struggled for more details, but none would come.

Each evening Josie shared with Max whatever she had remembered about herself that day. He listened intently, but made few comments.

What Josie did *not* mention was the memory of the purse she knew she'd had with her when she'd climbed onto the wagon with Rusty that first day on the Single C.

She knew she could broach the subject of the purse with Max without sounding as though she was accusing him of hiding it from her. She'd simply say she must have dropped it during the ride to wherever she'd gone, and could they travel that route slowly and look for it?

But she didn't.

Because she had no wish to find a purse holding the identification of who she was and where she lived. She didn't want to return to reality, leave the Single C and Max Carter.

Not yet.

This was stolen time, precious time, she told herself over and over. It would all end. Max and what they'd shared would become memories to be cherished during long, lonely nights in the future.

But not yet. Not yet.

On Halloween Max carved a huge pumpkin into a jack-o'-lantern. They delivered it to the Wilson children, who responded with shrieks of delight.

As Josie watched a smiling, laughing Max playing with the youngsters, a soft smile formed on her lips, and her heart felt as though it was melting like ice cream in the sun on a summer day.

"I told you," Sally said as the two women sat on the patio and sipped lemonade. "A whole different side of Max surfaces when he's with the kids."

"Yes, I can see that," Josie said. "It's beautiful."

"Josie," Sally said, looking directly at her, "are you falling in love with Max?"

Josie shifted her gaze to the ice cubes in the glass.

"I don't know," she said. "I don't *want* to know. I refuse to let myself find out. I'm remembering more each day, Sally. When it all comes back to me, I'll have to leave the Single C and Max. What's the point in discovering my true feelings for him?"

"Where is it etched in stone that you have to leave? Why can't you two consider having a future together? There's a gentleness, a peacefulness, about Max when he's with you.

"And the way he looks at you? Goodness, the man is crazy about you. It's written all over his face. Why, Josie? Why are you so certain you have to go and never return?"

Josie sighed and looked at Sally. "Max and I are so different, Sally. It's obvious from my clothes that I have money. How much or how I came by it, I don't know, but it would be a major stumbling block in a relationship with Max."

"That's a problem that could be solved," Sally said decisively.

"Then there's the way we approach life in general," Josie went on. "I'm a talker. I like to share my feelings, find out how other people view things and what's happened in their past to make them who they are today."

"That's reasonable. Lovers should be best friends, who share everything."

"Yes, but Max doesn't believe that. I never ask him personal questions, because he views it as an invasion of privacy. I don't know if he has ever been in love or why he's so dead set against getting married. I actually know more about myself now than I do about him, which isn't saying much."

"But you care about each other," Sally said.

"Anyone seeing you together could tell that in a second."

"That's true, but it's not deep enough, rich enough, to stand against the rigors of time. We're operating on the surface, because we both know this relationship is temporary. It's working for us, but it isn't real. It doesn't have a foundation of...well, forever."

"Darn that Max Carter," Sally said, shaking her head. "If he'd just lower those walls he's built around himself and share with you, bare his soul..."

"Sally, don't," Josie said quietly. "It isn't going to happen. I'll be leaving. I'll have to go."

"I hate this," Sally said. "I really hate this."

October slipped into November.

On the day Josie had been at the Single C for a month, she stared at the calendar, acutely aware that during those four weeks she hadn't had a period.

She splayed one hand on her flat stomach, wondering...

Was she carrying Max Carter's baby?

She waited for an emotional reaction to the unanswered question, but none came. Her mind, she realized, was refusing to address the issue right now. In the fantasy world where she was living with Max, the possibility of complications simply didn't exist.

Josie sighed and turned away from the calendar on the kitchen wall. She walked to the sink and stared out the window, absently noting the dark clouds building on the horizon.

Fantasy world, her mind echoed. Cinderella at the

ball, forgetting that the clock would strike at midnight.

Tick...tick...tick.

Today in a flash of renewed memory she'd seen an enormous house with beautifully maintained grounds. An elderly man had been standing on the wide porch, holding out his arms as though beckoning her to come to him.

Granddad.

She'd known that the man was her grandfather and that she called him Granddad. She had no parents. There were two brothers whose images faded in and out, never allowing her to see them clearly.

And once again the thought of brothers... No, it was more distinct than that. The thought of *one* of those brothers caused the now familiar chill to course throughout her.

These men were her family, and there was something wrong, something dark and ominous, connected to one of her brothers.

How could she have gone blissfully off to find an old school friend when there was something obviously upsetting or threatening her family? What had happened to that one brother to cause that cold fist to tighten within her whenever she had a fleeting thought of him?

Was she needed at home? Had she deserted her loved ones in a time of turmoil? Dear heaven, what kind of woman was she if she had actually done such a selfish act? Had she really decided to have a reunion with Max's cousin, Sabrina, instead of standing by her family as she should have?

Tick...tick...tick.

"Oh, God," she said pressing trembling fingertips to her lips.

The clock was going to strike midnight. Her wonderful fantasy life with Max was about to end. She had to search her mind harder for details about herself, her Granddad, her brothers.

She had to discover who she was.

She had to go home.

And leave Max.

Forever.

Josie blinked away sudden tears, then turned from the window. She checked the roast in the oven, which she'd prepared as per Max's instructions.

She was actually learning how to cook, she thought, striving to push away the depression setting over her. She was turning into a Henrietta Housewife. She enjoyed getting the evening meal on the table, but still had no enthusiasm for cleaning the house.

She picked up four of Max's shirts from the table and headed down the hall to hang the freshly washed garments in his closet. She'd instinctively known how to operate the washer and dryer the first time she'd stood in front of the machines with a laundry basket of clothes.

In the bedroom she removed hangers from the closet and placed the shirts on the bed, smoothing them onto the hangers one at a time.

It was all coming together, she thought. The man she knew as Granddad had raised her and her brothers in that huge home. And she had no doubt that a housekeeper had done all the cooking and cleaning.

At some point she'd moved to the place high above the ground that was peaceful, inviting...and hers. It was there that she'd probably taken on the chore of washing her own clothes, but hadn't bothered to learn how to cook.

Someone must come in to clean the spacious, airy rooms she called home. Yes, she'd arranged for that to be done, because she was wealthy and had grown up surrounded by opulence in the big house with her Granddad. She took money for granted, because it had always been there.

Strange, Josie thought, glancing around Max's small bedroom. She was so comfortable here in this shabby little house. It was cozy, wrapped itself around her like a warm blanket.

And Max lived here.

He came in each evening, dirty and sweaty...and smiling. Oh, yes, Max Carter smiled a great deal now. It softened his rugged features and lit up the dark pools of his eyes.

On three different occasions he'd brought her wildflowers that he'd found blooming late in the season.

Another day he'd delayed his chores to take her to the barn to witness the miracle of kittens being born.

One sunny afternoon, he'd come in early, saddled a horse, settled Josie on its back and led the animal around and around the corral. She had laughed in delight and hung on for dear life.

Little by little, Max had revealed the softer, gentler side of himself, the caring, thoughtful man who made no attempt to hide the fact that he was very glad to see her at day's end.

She still knew nothing about his childhood, his past, but nevertheless, Max seemed to be stepping out from behind his protective walls. He was warm, loving and lovable.

Lovable?

Was she falling in love with Max?

Tick...tick...tick.

Don't think about that, Josie, she told herself, walking to the closet with the hangers. There was no point in knowing.

Max still refused to share himself totally.

The differences in their life-styles screamed the fact that they had no future.

There was only the present, the here and now, and time was running out.

Tick...tick...tick.

Josie hung up the shirts, then tsked in disgust as one slipped from the hanger and fell to the floor. She bent over to retrieve it, lost her balance and dropped to her knees.

"Very graceful, Josie," she said aloud.

As she reached for the shirt, she caught sight of something in the back of the closet that made her heart thunder. With a shaking hand she pulled out a tapestry purse with a leather shoulder strap.

This was *her* purse, she thought frantically. The moment she'd touched it she'd known it was hers, the one she'd had with her in the memory of climbing onto the wagon seat with Rusty.

Max had hidden her purse from her.

Max Carter had lied to her.

A sob caught in her throat as she unzipped the purse and snatched out the soft, leather wallet. Tears slid down her pale cheeks as she opened the wallet and stared at the driver's license.

"Josie Wentworth," she whispered, tears nearly choking off her words. "I'm Josie Wentworth. I'm twenty-nine years old. I live in Freemont Springs. Oh, God, Max, why? Why did you lie to me?"

She dropped the wallet and stumbled to her feet.

She had to get out of the house. It was crashing down around her from the weight of Max's lies, crushing her.

Josie ran, hardly able to see through her tears. Down the hall, across the living room, through the kitchen, then out the back door, she ran.

Away...away...away.

She had to get away from the crumbling house of lies.

Chapter Eight

Max swung into the cab of the truck and headed back toward the house, glancing often at the darkening sky. The wind was picking up, accompanied by the deep rumble of thunder.

They were in for a beaut of a storm, he thought as he was jostled by the rutted ground. It was one of those fast-moving babies that seemed to come out of nowhere in a big rush to do as much damage as possible.

Was Josie afraid of thunder and lightning? He didn't know, but he was moving as quickly as he could to be with her, just in case she became frightened when the building fury of the storm cut loose.

Josie, Josie, Josie, his mind echoed. Damn, these weeks with her had been sensational. She greeted him with a smile and a kiss whenever he entered the house, and he had to admit he was equally glad to see *her.*

He quit working a bit earlier each day now so he wasn't dead tired and could spend the evening with Josie in the living room. They chatted, never running out of things to talk about, even though they cut a wide berth around personal subjects.

That was proof positive that two people could be together night after night without dissecting the issues of each other's past. Josie was definitely learning the important difference between sharing and invading a person's privacy.

And the lovemaking with Josie?

Instantly, heated desire coiled low within Max and he chuckled.

He'd better not think about the lovemaking or he'd lose control too soon. He'd wait until Josie was in his arms before he gave way to the passion that was always just a hairbreadth away from being ignited into hot flames.

Josie seemed very happy on the Single C, comfortable in his crummy little house. Her smiles were real; he knew they were, because they reached the depths of her beautiful eyes.

He'd been surprised as hell when she'd tackled the mess in the front yard. It was looking really nice, and Josie seemed to get a great deal of pleasure and satisfaction from the project.

A wealthy, jet-set Wentworth who didn't mind getting dirty? Amazing.

The only tense moments he had after coming in at day's end were when Josie told him how much of her memory had returned that day. He'd let out a pent-up breath of relief each time it was apparent that she hadn't recalled who she was.

Which meant she wasn't planning to leave him.

Not yet.

Because the bottom line was, he didn't want Josie to go.

Not yet.

Max frowned as the house, barn and other buildings came into view.

Was he falling in love with Josie? he asked himself. No, forget it. He didn't want to know. She would eventually drive away from the Single C.

From where he was he could see her expensive car where he'd hidden it behind the shed farthest from the house. Rusty knew why the car was there and had assured Max he'd tell the hands it was none of their dang business if they inquired about the vehicle. Since Josie never ventured far from the house, there was little chance of her finding the car.

But, yes, Josie would leave. That was a given. It served no purpose to determine how he really felt about her. He'd just hang fast to his belief that he didn't want a wife and family, and enjoy the remaining hours with Josie as they unfolded.

When it was over—when she left—he'd be fine, simply resume his life as it had been before the day she'd appeared on his spread. No problem.

He just didn't want her to go *now*.

Max parked the truck close to the barn at the very moment the sky opened and cold rain descended in a wind-whipped torrent. He got out of the truck, slammed the door and was drenched to the skin within seconds.

"Hell," he muttered.

"We're going to get it good," Rusty yelled from the doorway to the barn.

"Yeah," Max hollered. "Have you got the horses under control?"

Rusty nodded. "Never a doubt about it, boss. Never a doubt."

Max waved a hand in acknowledgment, then took off at a run toward the house, splashing mud on his boots and jeans from puddles already forming on the ground.

He barreled through the back door of the house and teetered slightly as he came to an abrupt halt, dripping dirty water onto the kitchen floor.

"Josie!" he called. "Hey, where are you? Hiding under the bed because of the storm? I've come to rescue you, just like a hero in a book. Josie?"

Silence was his only answer.

"Josie?" He started forward, oblivious to the fact that he was tracking mud. "Josie, come on. This isn't funny. Where are you?"

He strode down the hall and into his bedroom—then stopped dead in his tracks. His heart began beating so rapidly he could hear the wild tempo in his ears.

Josie's purse and wallet lay on the floor in front of the open closet door.

"No," he said, a frantic edge to his voice. "Ah, damn it, no!"

He turned and raced back down the hall, looking

quickly into the second bedroom before continuing on to the living room. He stopped, staring at the front door.

Had Josie called a taxi? Had she left the ranch in a cab? No, no, that didn't add up. She might have been upset enough to leave her clothes behind, but she would have taken the purse he'd hidden in the back of the closet.

That meant...

Dear God, that meant Josie had been so devastated when she'd discovered her purse she'd fled on foot.

Josie was out there somewhere in the storm.

Max charged out the back door, hardly able to see three feet in front of him because of the driving rain. He cupped his hands around his mouth.

"Jo-o-o-sie!" he yelled.

But all he heard were the taunting sounds of the rain and wind.

Josie ran until her lungs burned and her vision was blurred by tears. She entered the woods at the far side of Max's land and dropped to her knees, covering her face with her hands and weeping.

Max had lied to her.

It had all been a game to him, a sadistic, cruel scheme to keep her on the Single C and in his bed.

Lies, all lies.

The wind invaded the woods, rustling the brightly colored leaves on the trees. Josie stilled and lifted her head, not moving, hardly breathing, as she listened intently.

"The song of autumn," she whispered as tears

glistened on her pale cheeks. "Granddad. Michael. Jack." The familiar chill coursed through her. "Jack. Oh, God, Jack is dead. My brother, my beloved Jack, is dead."

Like a movie playing in her mind, it all came back, picture by picture, frame by frame. The ring in the blue velvet box. The letter. Sabrina Jensen. And the return of her memory was accompanied by the cold, painful truth of Max Carter's deception.

She hadn't come to the Single C to find an old school friend. Sabrina Jensen was, quite possibly, the woman her brother had fallen in love with and wished to marry. If that was true, then she'd wanted to welcome Sabrina into the Wentworth family.

There had also been the hope that Sabrina might bring at least a modicum of comfort to Joseph Wentworth by talking about the man they'd both loved so dearly.

And Max knew that, because she'd carefully explained exactly why she had come to the Single C. But Max had refused to help her, arguing that she was invading Sabrina's privacy by stepping into areas that were none of her business.

And then, when she'd been vulnerable with amnesia, he'd devised a plan to teach her a lesson and to keep her on his ranch, while refusing to divulge anything about himself.

Come into my bed, Josie, but stay the hell out of my heart, mind and soul.

She'd gone along with it, believed all the stark and cruel lies, while Max no doubt struggled to keep from laughing aloud at her gullibility.

She hadn't made love with Max Carter. She'd had sex with a stranger, a man she'd never really known.

Now she felt as though her heart was shattering into a million pieces.

Josie wrapped her hands around her elbows and rocked back and forth, giving way once again to tears. Rain—cold, biting rain—began to fall, but she didn't care.

She simply cried for all that she'd lost, all that she'd never really had—with Max.

Joseph Wentworth banged the top of the desk in his library with one fist and glared at the man standing on the opposite side of the gleaming, massive piece of furniture.

"Damn it, Mason," Joseph said. "You'd better have something to report today. You're supposedly the best detective in these parts. I hired you three weeks ago to find my granddaughter. So far, you haven't told me a damn thing, other than that Josie bought some pastries and a soft drink on the way out of town, heading for Muskogee."

"I realize that, sir," the detective said. "But we had a big area to cover. We came up zero on hotels, motels, hospitals and—"

"I know that," Joseph interrupted.

"That left the ranch country," Mason said. "It's been slow going, sir, but I have some positive news for you today."

Joseph sat up straighter in his chair, his heart pounding.

"Spit it out, man," he said gruffly.

"One of my people was questioning a bartender in a place where a lot of cowboys hang out. A ranch hand from a spread called the Single C—it's owned by a Max Carter—spoke up and said there was a car matching the description of Josie's parked behind a shed on the ranch, and it had been there for several weeks. My man just called in that news to me. He's headed for the Single C right now."

"Dear God," Joseph whispered.

"The thing is, sir, there's a big storm raging in that section. That's why so many cowboys were in the bar during the day. They'd been sent home from the ranches to get out of the storm. My man isn't certain the back-country roads are still passable. He may have to sit out the storm before he can get into the Single C. He said he'd get back to me and let me know."

"The hell he will," Joseph said, rising to his feet. "You're coming with me, Mason. We're driving there ourselves. Right now."

"But—"

"I'll get onto the Single C Ranch if I have to buy a boat and row in. You call your man in his vehicle and arrange for a place for us to meet. If that *is* Josie's car, Max Carter is going to answer *my* questions face-to-face. By damn, he'll be dealing with Joseph Wentworth."

Max urged his horse forward, the animal moving slowly through the mud. The wind howled, swirling the cold rain into a frenzy.

Rusty had offered to help search for Josie; he'd

asked no questions about why she was out in the storm. Max had refused to allow Rusty to accompany him, because the danger of being struck by lightning on the open range was far too great.

He'd been looking for Josie for more than an hour now, calling her name into the wind until his throat was raw. He could hardly see beyond the horse's head as the rain pelted down like stinging, physical blows.

Ah, Josie, he thought frantically, where are you? If anything happened to her, he'd— No, he wasn't going to think along those lines. She was out here somewhere, wet, cold, terribly upset, but she wasn't injured.

"Josie!" he yelled. The wind tore her name from his lips.

This was all his fault. He'd set the lies in motion to keep from being sued by the wealthy Wentworths. He'd continued the string of lies because he hadn't wanted Josie to leave him.

Would she ever understand why he'd done what he had? Would she forgive him? Would she agree to sit down and hear him out?

Lord, he hoped so. The thought of her walking out of his life with the pain of betrayal radiating from her big, brown eyes was more than he could deal with.

Come on, Carter, he thought, swiping the rain from his face. The important thing now was to find Josie, get her safely out of this storm and home where she belonged.

Home where she belonged? his mind echoed. In

his house? In that shabby little structure Josie had filled to overflowing with her sunshine smile and wind-chime laughter?

No. Cripes, no. He didn't want anything permanent with Josie Wentworth. No commitment, no strings, had been the agreement they'd made, the rules they'd been following for the past month.

Besides, once Josie realized how much money she had, she'd turn her pretty little Wentworth nose up at the sight of his crummy house and his backwoods ranch. Josie would leave the Single C just as they'd both known she would. He just didn't want her hurt and hating him when she left. He didn't want to be the cause of her tears.

"Josie!" Max yelled again.

He reached the woods at the far edge of his land and swung out of the saddle. It was dangerous enough to be on a horse on the open range in a lightning storm. He sure wasn't riding into tall trees while high in the saddle.

Leading the horse by the reins, Max made his way forward, the branches of trees whipping painfully against his body.

"Josie! Where are you, Josie?"

Josie lifted her head and uncurled herself from her huddled position beneath the low-hanging branches of a tree.

Max? Had she heard his voice, or had that been only the wind, howling, taunting her into believing that Max had come for her?

She was hopelessly lost and terribly frightened. A

part of her never wanted to see Max Carter again. Another part prayed he would search for her, wouldn't give up until he found her and took her home.

Home? No, Max's house wasn't her home. She lived in a penthouse apartment in Freemont Springs. It was lush and plush, expensively furnished, a place where she'd never dream of entering with hands muddied from pulling weeds. It was who she was, where she belonged.

The clock had struck midnight.

It was time to go home.

Tick...tick...tick.

"Josie!"

She scrambled to her feet, her heart racing.

That was Max's voice, she thought frantically. She was positive. Oh, thank God, he'd come for her. She had to find him before he gave up and went looking for her somewhere else.

"Max!" she hollered, stumbling forward. "Max, I'm here. Please, Max, please, I'm here!"

Max stopped statue-still, straining his ears, squinting against the pelting rain.

He'd heard Josie. She'd called his name. That hadn't been the keening wind, had it? No, it was Josie. It had to be. She was in these woods and, by damn, he was going to find her.

He pushed aside tree branches, still calling her name.

Seconds seemed like hours.

And then...

"Max!"

Josie burst through the trees a hundred yards ahead of him, barely visible through the rain.

She tripped and fell, disappearing from his sight.

Max dropped the reins and ran in the direction he'd seen her.

Josie struggled to her feet, the fleeting image she'd had of Max giving her the energy to surge forward.

Then it all seemed to happen in slow motion.

Lightning zigzagged across the sky like an angry monster reaching out with dangerous, sharp claws to claim its prey.

With an earsplitting crack the lightning slammed into a tree, toppling it as though it was no more than a toothpick.

The frightened horse reared, then turned and bolted away.

The tree began to fall....

"No!" Josie screamed.

The tree struck Max, throwing him to the ground.

Trapping him beneath its weight.

Chapter Nine

Josie ran.

She halted for a heart-stopping moment to stare at Max with wide, horrified eyes. He was on his back, eyes closed, not moving.

She tugged at the branches of the tree, a sob escaping from her lips as wet leaves tore away and filled her shaking hands.

"Max?" she cried. "Oh, God, Max, can you hear me? I'll get help. I'll be back with help, I promise. Just hang on, Max."

Her bone-deep fatigue forgotten, she raced out of the woods and started across the wet, muddy, open range. Thunder rumbled and lightning crackled in the dark sky, but the rain had slackened enough for her to see where she was going. With instincts coming from a place she couldn't identify, she headed for the ranch house. She could use the telephone to call for help for Max.

She tripped and fell, splashing into a hole of dirty water, then she dragged herself to her feet, tears joining the rain on her face.

Her lungs burned and her legs threatened to give way beneath her. But she ran on, repeating Max's name over and over in her mind like a mantra.

At last the house and barn came into view. The rain had diminished to a light drizzle, and she staggered forward, gasping for breath as she riveted her gaze on the back door of the house.

A hundred feet…fifty…twenty more feet to go.…

Josie burst through the back door, instantly losing her footing and sprawling facedown on the floor with a sharp cry of pain.

"Josie!"

She raised her head. "Granddad!"

Josie scrambled to her feet and launched herself at Joseph, hugging him tightly. He wrapped his arms around her, oblivious to the wet mud covering his expensive suit.

Josie moved back and clutched the lapels of her grandfather's suit jacket.

"Oh, Granddad, please," she said, fresh tears spilling onto her dirty cheeks. "You've got to help Max. He came looking for me because I… It's all my fault that he's hurt and…a tree in the woods…the lightning… Granddad, please, Max is pinned beneath a tree. He's unconscious, but he's alive, and I promised him I'd get help for him. Please, Granddad, please. I love him. He's my Max. Please, you've got to—''

Joseph gripped her shoulders and gave her a small shake. ''Josie,'' he said sternly, ''calm down. Take a deep breath. Are you all right?''

''Yes, yes, I'm fine, but Max—''

''Why didn't you contact me? What's going on here?''

''I bumped my head and had amnesia. Granddad, I'll explain everything later. Max is hurt, don't you understand?''

''Yes, I hear you,'' Joseph said, nodding. ''I *will* have the answers to all my questions, but first things first.'' He released Josie and turned toward the living room. ''Rusty, Mason, get in here. We have an emergency situation on our hands. I want my orders followed to the letter. Snap to it. *Now.*''

Josie lowered herself onto a chair in the Muskogee-hospital waiting room and watched absently as her grandfather shook the hands of the four members of the Search and Rescue Unit. The diminishing fury of the storm had made it possible for the unit to come to the Single C by helicopter. They'd picked up Joseph and Josie, then flown to the edge of the woods where Josie directed them.

Instructed to stay in the helicopter after telling the men where Max lay injured in the woods, Josie waited for what seemed like an eternity before seeing the group emerge from the woods with Max on a stretcher.

She'd sat next to a still-unconscious Max during

the flight to Muskogee, holding his hand, staring at his scratched and bleeding face.

At the hospital, Max had been whisked away, his hand torn from hers.

Exhaustion fell over her like a heavy shroud, making it difficult to breathe. She leaned her head back against the wall and closed her eyes, telling herself to inhale, exhale, inhale—

"Well, we've done all we can," Joseph said, sitting down in the chair next to her. "It's up to the doctors now. Josie, here—drink this tea."

Josie opened her eyes and reached for the plastic cup with a trembling hand. She sipped the hot liquid, feeling its soothing warmth flow through her.

Joseph waited until he saw some color return to her face beneath the streaks of dirt. He frowned as he flicked at the dried mud on his suit, then gave up the attempt to make himself presentable.

"Well, Princess," he said, "let's start at the beginning, shall we?"

"Oh, Granddad, not now, please. I'm so exhausted and so very worried about Max. Couldn't we discuss all this later?"

"No."

Josie sighed, drained the cup, then placed it on the table next to her.

"What do you want to know?" she said.

"Everything."

A bubble of near-hysterical laughter escaped from her lips.

Everything? she thought. No, her darling granddad did *not* want to hear about the exquisite lovemaking his precious Princess had shared with Max Carter. In Joseph Wentworth's eyes she was still his little girl. There were definitely some details of this bizarre story she was going to leave out.

"Josie," Joseph said, an edge of impatience in his voice, "I've put in a hellish month worrying about you. I had enough to deal with because of Jack's death. I find nothing funny about this situation, young lady. I want my answers and I want them right now."

"Yes, of course, I'm sorry." Josie straightened in her chair and drew a steadying breath. "Okay, here goes. When I returned to my apartment after my stay with you, I found a box of Jack's personal effects that Trey McGill had mailed to me."

Joseph propped his elbows on the arms of the chair, made a steeple of his fingers and rested his hands against his lips. He stared straight ahead as he listened.

"Among Jack's things," Josie went on, "was a letter addressed to a Sabrina Jensen, care of Max Carter at the Single C Ranch, a picture of Sabrina and a diamond ring in a blue velvet box."

"What?" Joseph said, looking at her.

"I read the letter," Josie said, "but I wasn't certain from what Jack wrote whether or not he was in love with Sabrina and planned to ask her to marry him."

"Marry? Jack?"

"I know, Granddad. It was hard for me to believe, too. But if Jack *was* in love with Sabrina, I felt she should be made to feel welcome in our family. Plus, you could have talked to her, shared things about Jack. I didn't want to get your hopes up, though, so I decided to talk to Sabrina myself before I told you about her."

"I see." Joseph resumed his earlier pose, staring straight ahead. "Go on."

"I found the Single C Ranch and Max Carter, but Sabrina wasn't there. Then I apparently—I don't remember exactly—fell in a hole made by a tree stump that Max had removed from the ground. I hit my head and wound up with amnesia."

"I'll sue him," Joseph said tightly. "That cowboy can kiss his postage-stamp-size ranch goodbye."

"You'll do no such thing," Josie said, her voice rising. "It wasn't Max's fault that I fell in the stupid hole. I was in one of my snits and... You will *not* sue Max Carter, Granddad or give even a fleeting thought to taking his ranch from him. That land is his life, his reason for being. It would destroy him if you—"

"Enough," Joseph said, flicking one hand in the air. "I was just checking. I won't sue Max Carter."

"Checking what?" Josie said, confused.

"Nothing. Continue."

She shrugged. "There's not much else to say. I was regaining my memory in bits and pieces, but I still didn't know who I was until today."

"Josie, you must have introduced yourself when you first met Carter. Plus, you were carrying a purse with all kinds of identification.

"In addition, I was able to locate you because a ranch hand acknowledged your car as being the one that had been behind a shed on the Single C for several weeks.

"Max Carter obviously knew who you were the entire time you had amnesia. He deliberately chose not to tell you your identity. Why?"

Josie lifted her chin. "Granddad, I don't know why, but I intend to find out. I'm asking you—no, correct that—I'm *telling* you to step back and let me pursue this on my own. It's between me and Max."

Joseph coughed, and Josie had the impression he did it to hide a smile. But what on earth was he smiling about?

"Fine," he said.

Josie's eyes widened. "Fine? Just like that? No argument? No renewed threats to sue Max? Take away his ranch?"

"No."

"Why not?" she said, eyeing him warily. "This isn't like you at all, Granddad."

"I'm mellowing in my old age."

"Ha!"

A nurse stepped into the room.

"Max?" Josie jumped to her feet.

"No," the nurse said. "There's no word yet on his condition. There's a telephone call at the nurses' station for Mr. Wentworth."

"Oh." Josie sat back down on her chair with a weary sigh.

Joseph followed the nurse to the station and picked up the receiver.

"Wentworth."

"Mason. I ran a quick check on Max Carter like you asked me to. He's squeaky clean, dull as dishwater. The guy has a mortgage on his land, no other outstanding bills, has never even had a traffic ticket."

"Excellent," Joseph said. "You're still at the Single C?"

"Yes."

"Stay there until you hear from me. Pack Josie's belongings, but don't leave until I find out Carter's condition."

"Yes, sir."

Joseph hung up the receiver and allowed a full-blown smile to break across his face as he returned to the waiting room.

Twenty minutes later Jeff Wilson came striding into the waiting room.

"Jeff!" Josie jumped instantly to her feet. "How did you know—"

"Rusty called the house and Sally had me paged here. I was in to see one of my patients. Are you all right, Josie? You look like you fought in a war."

"Yes, I'm fine. My memory's fully restored, too. Jeff, please, how is Max?"

"Joseph Wentworth," Joseph interrupted, extending his hand to Jeff when he reached Josie's side. "I'm Josie's grandfather. She's forgetting her manners, I'm afraid."

"Dr. Jeff Wilson," Jeff said, shaking Joseph's hand. "I treated your granddaughter when she received that bump on the head."

Joseph nodded. "Send me a bill."

"Max took care of it," Jeff said.

"Jeff!" Josie was nearly yelling. "How is Max?"

"He is one very lucky man. *He* doesn't think that's true at the moment, but he really is fortunate. The ground was so wet that it cushioned the impact when the tree hit him. He sort of sank into the mud and didn't get the full force of the tree's weight."

"And?" Josie clutched her hands together tightly.

"He has a concussion, which, as you well know, means he has a roaring headache. His ribs are badly bruised and very sore. But the thing that has him hopping mad is that his right leg is broken."

Josie's eyes shimmered with tears. "Max has a broken leg? Oh, that's terrible, just awful."

"Not when you consider that he's lucky to be alive," Jeff said.

"Well, yes," she said slowly. "If you look at it that way, I guess he—"

"Is he bedridden?" Joseph asked.

Jeff nodded. "Indeed he is. I'm going to have to see about getting a nurse out to the Single C to tend to him for a while, until that leg has healed enough for a walking cast. I told Max he couldn't get of bed, then hightailed it from the room before he could get his hands around my throat. He'd probably be bellowing right now, except that his head and ribs hurt too much for him to holler."

Jeff chuckled. "Max is fuming silently," he added, smiling. "He's sort of like a volcano waiting to erupt."

"May I see him?" Josie asked.

"You're a brave lady, Josie. But, sure, you can

say hello to him. Don't stay too long, though. He needs to rest and he's looking at a night of being poked awake to check on that concussion. He's down the hall. Third door on the right."

"Thank you, Jeff, for everything. Oh, and please tell Sally that I said goodbye and it was wonderful spending time with her. I'll be returning to Freemont Springs with my grandfather."

"We'll miss you, Josie," Jeff said.

"Thank you. I'll miss you, too. Goodbye."

Josie hurried from the room and Jeff turned to do the same.

"Wait a second, Jeff," Joseph said. "I'd like to speak with you, if I may?"

"Certainly, sir. What can I do for you?"

"Come sit down," Joseph said, placing one arm across Jeff's shoulders. "I have a proposition to make."

On the way to Max's room, Josie ducked into a bathroom, grimacing as she saw her mud-splattered face in the mirror. She scrubbed off the dirt with a wet paper towel, finger-combed her hair, then sighed in defeat.

Why was she concerned about her appearance? Max Carter was a rotten liar, a miscreant, a self-serving, conniving...

She sighed again.

Then there was the flip side of the coin. If she had stayed in the house and confronted Max with the discovery of her purse, he wouldn't be hurt. But oh, no, she'd gone running off like a child throwing a tantrum and Max had come after her, resulting in his injuries.

Good grief, this was confusing.

A part of her wanted to call Max every name in the book, then tell him to go straight to hell.

Another part of her was eager to apologize for being the cause of his current condition.

Well, she'd wing it. Just wait and see what came out of her mouth when she saw him. She was far too exhausted to think it through or decide on a plan of action.

All she knew for certain was that she had to see Max one last time before she left for Freemont Springs. Before she walked out of his life forever.

Outside the room Jeff had directed her to, Josie drew a steadying breath, lifted her chin, then rapped lightly on the door before pushing it open.

Max was sleeping, his dark lashes fanned out against tanned skin that had a gray hue in the glow of the small light above the bed.

His face had a multitude of nasty scratches and bruises. A tented blanket was above his right leg, the leg broken because of her childish behavior.

"Max?" she said softly. "Max?"

He opened his eyes and her breath caught as she saw the physical pain radiating from their dark depths.

"Oh, Max," she said, fighting against threatening tears. "I'm so sorry, so very sorry. This is all my fault. Can you ever forgive me?"

"Forgive *you?*" he said, then moaned and splayed one hand on his chest. "Damn. Josie, *I* should be asking for *your* forgiveness. I was the one who concealed your identity from you."

"There is that," she said, frowning. "You definitely owe me an explanation, Max Carter. On the other hand, maybe not. There's nothing you could say to... It was a despicable thing to do and... Then again, I feel just terrible about what happened to you when you came into the woods and—"

Joseph Wentworth came into the room without bothering to knock on the door.

"Max Carter?" he said, stopping at the foot of the bed. "I'm Joseph Wentworth, Josie's grandfather."

"Oh, hell," Max said, rolling his eyes heavenward. "Let me guess. You're going to sue my butt."

"Sue you?" Joseph said, raising his eyebrow. "Whatever for? My dear boy, I'm in your debt for what you did for my precious Princess."

"What?" Josie and Max said in unison.

"Heavens, yes," Joseph said, smiling. "Why, there Josie was with no memory, no way to know she could contact me to come for her, and you provided her with a safe haven. A port in the storm, if you will."

"Hold it," Josie said, raising one hand. "Granddad, this man *concealed* my identity from me. He hid my purse with all my identification in the back of his closet, for crying out loud."

"I'm sure there's a reasonable explanation for that, Josie," Joseph said. "But we don't want to tire Max out by demanding to know what it is at the present time."

"We don't?" Josie said, planting her hands on her hips. "Yes, we do. We most certainly do."

"The fact remains," her grandfather said, glaring at her, "that you were safely tucked away with Max on the Single C while you had no idea who you were. You could have been wandering around the streets of Muskogee or somewhere. The very thought gives me cold chills. I intend to repay Max for his kindness to you."

"But—"

"Therefore," Joseph went on, "I've just had a lengthy conversation with Jeff. Tomorrow Max will be flown by air ambulance to Freemont Springs. I'll also make arrangements to have extra ranch hands sent out to the Single C to tend to the chores under Rusty's direction. Those men will be paid by me, of course. It's the least I can do.

"Wentworths always pay their debts, Josie. You'd do well to remember that."

"Meaning?" she said, narrowing her eyes.

"Max cared for you when you suffered the injury to your head. It's time to reciprocate. Max will be settled comfortably in your apartment until the day he is able to return to work on his ranch."

"The hell I will!" Max exclaimed, then groaned in pain.

"That's crazy!" Josie shrieked.

"What it is," Joseph said, "is settled. Max, your personal physician is writing the orders in your chart right now. You have no choice, really, but to accept my heartfelt offer. A private nurse staying at the Single C would be a strain on your finances that, quite frankly, you can't afford."

"But I don't want to have Max there," Josie nearly sputtered.

"You're a Wentworth, who is beholden to this man for your well-being. You'll set that debt to rights. Understood?"

"I..." Josie said.

"Good."

Joseph strode out of the room.

"I don't believe this." Josie shook her head. "I do *not* believe this."

"All I know," Max said, "is that your grandfather doesn't plan to sue me and that the Single C is being taken care of properly." He nodded. "That's enough to satisfy me—at least in my present condition." He closed his eyes. "Go home, Josie. I have a rotten headache."

"But—"

Max opened one eye. "Oh, and be certain everything is ready for me, Florence Nightingale. I'm arriving on your doorstep tomorrow."

Josie spun on her heel and marched from the room.

Max frowned as he watched her go. He'd handled that like a cocky so-and-so, he thought. Nicely done. He didn't have the energy to figure out how he actually felt about this bizarre turn of events, so he'd gone for being obnoxious.

What little oomph he had left was centered on one very disturbing question.

What in the hell was Joseph Wentworth up to?

Chapter Ten

Max opened his eyes halfway, then stifled the groan gathering force in his chest.

He had, he decided, what felt like a hangover, worse than any he'd suffered during his younger, rowdier days.

Darn that Jeff Wilson. His so-called buddy had taken it upon himself to knock him out cold with an enormous shot for pain, before allowing him to undertake the flight to Freemont Springs, then the ambulance trip to Josie's.

There'd be a ride in an elevator, as well, Jeff had said, since Josie lived in a penthouse apartment. And all that jostling would be agony for a man in his condition, Jeff had announced cheerfully before saying, "Sleep tight, Carter."

"Damn," Max said, squeezing his temples with one hand, "I'm dying."

He'd better think about something other than his killer headache.

He opened his eyes the rest of the way, slowly, cautiously, and began to scrutinize the large room where he was lying in a double bed with an intricately carved oak headboard.

White carpeting? *White?* Josie sure wasn't planning on some grungy cowboy tromping through this place in muddy boots. No way. The people who entered Ms. Wentworth's penthouse apartment knew what mud was, but had probably never touched the stuff.

Oh, man, what in the hell was he doing here? He was so out of his league, so far from the world where he belonged, it was a crime. Just looking around Josie's room made him feel big and clumsy, and too rough, with his bulky muscles and callused hands. White carpeting. Cripes.

This, he thought, was where Josie lived day in, day out, where she was comfortable and at ease. It made it even more unbelievable that she'd stayed so long on the Single C in his shabby house, seemingly content.

Of course, he reasoned, she hadn't known at the time who she was or that a plush apartment like this was waiting for her in Freemont Springs.

But one would think that a lifetime of having been surrounded by the finest, of having people wait on her hand and foot, would have caused her subconscious to send messages of revulsion regarding where she was residing.

He'd bet his best cow horse that Josie was now shaking her head in wonder that she'd survived the ordeal at the primitive Single C.

Their lovemaking sure as hell hadn't been an ordeal, though, Max thought, sliding one arm beneath his head on the pillow. It had been sensational, incredible. Like nothing he'd ever experienced before.

He felt a coiling of desire as scenes of making love with Josie began to materialize in his mind's eye.

"Knock it off, Carter," he muttered. What he'd do well to concentrate on was why Joseph Wentworth had been so hell-bent on installing him in his granddaughter's guest room. Why would someone like Joseph Wentworth deposit an uncivilized, poor-as-a-church-mouse cowboy in his precious Princess's megabucks apartment?

It hadn't made sense yesterday. It didn't make sense now. Well, he wanted an answer to that question and he fully intended to get it.

That Josie owed him, had a debt to repay was pure bull. Joseph knew that Max had withheld his granddaughter's true identity from her. Why wasn't the man suing him, or even getting him slapped in jail?

This whole scenario was crazy.

Max's stomach rumbled and he turned his head to look at the clock on the nightstand. It was two in the afternoon. He'd slept most of the day away. No wonder he was famished.

So now what? His lousy broken leg meant he couldn't go strolling into the kitchen to raid the refrigerator. Hell, he was actually a prisoner in this bed, this room, this apartment.

Was that it? Did Joseph have a diabolical plan to get revenge by having him lie here and slowly starve to death? Was he alone in the apartment, Josie having been whisked away to somewhere else by her grandfather?

How did they intend to dispose of his body when he croaked?

Money. Money could buy anything, including silence about the poor sucker who died of starvation in Josie Wentworth's apartment. Well, by damn, he wasn't checking out without a fight.

"Help!" Max yelled, clutching his painful ribs. "Someone. Anyone. Help!"

Josie's head snapped up, her concentration on preparing a tray of food for Max broken.

Help? she thought. Max wasn't calling her name; he was hollering for anyone, someone for help? Dear heaven, was he delirious?

Josie ran down the hall and into the guest bedroom, where a sleeping Max had been settled into bed hours before by the ambulance attendants.

"What? What?" she said, coming to a teetering halt next to the bed.

"Aha," Max said, pointing a finger at her. "You haven't left yet, huh? Well, I want you to know that I'm wise to you and your vengeful grandfather's master plan. It won't work, you know. I'll get out of this apartment even if I have to drag myself inch by inch along the floor."

Josie placed her hand on Max's forehead. "You don't have a fever," she murmured. "You must be out of your head from that shot Jeff gave you."

"Help!" Max bellowed.

"Would you cut that out?" Josie said, cringing. "You're going to crack the plaster in the ceiling. Just hush and wait for the effects of the drug to wear off."

"They've already worn off," Max said none too quietly. "I'm being held prisoner here. I'm at your mercy. You're going to starve me to death, right? Your grandfather decided that taking my ranch or putting me in jail wasn't enough punishment. You two decided I should die slowly."

"What?" Josie said, bursting into laughter. "Good grief, Max. You've been watching too many horror movies. I was fixing you a tray of food when you started yelling your head off." She paused and frowned. "Of course, with my lack of culinary talents, I suppose that could be viewed as a slow death."

"You were preparing me a meal?"

"Yes."

"Oh." Max nodded. "Well, maybe my imagination got a little carried away."

"More than a little," Josie said, rolling her eyes.

"All right, I'm sorry, but let's cut to the chase, shall we? Josie, why am I here? Your grandfather's bull about you owing me is a crock, and you know it. Why isn't he fuming over the fact that I concealed your identity from you?"

Josie sighed. "I don't know, Max. When I pressed

Granddad on the subject, he asked me if I remembered what I'd said when I came barreling into your house from the woods after you were struck by the tree."

"And?"

"It's a blur. I was totally exhausted and hysterical, begging him to get help for you but..." She shrugged. "I'm trying to recall what else I said, but I don't have the slightest clue at this point."

Max frowned. "But Joseph's attitude, his determination that I recuperate here hinges on something you said when you first saw him?"

"Apparently so."

"Then think! What did you say?"

"I don't remember!" Josie said, flinging out her arms.

"Cripes."

"You're getting very grumpy," Josie said, turning and starting toward the bedroom door. "I'll bring you something to eat. Maybe that will improve your mood."

"I doubt it," Max muttered under his breath.

"I heard that, Carter," she said as she disappeared from view. "Food is food. What I fix won't be great, but it will fill your stomach. So shut up!"

Max chuckled at Josie's snippy retort. Oh, yes, he thought, she was really something, Ms. Feisty Wentworth.

In the next moment Max sobered.

Fighting against tremendous obstacles, Josie had managed to get help for him when he'd been struck by that tree. She'd had to have been exhausted already from running to the woods from the house after discovering her purse hidden in the closet.

But despite her fatigue and the danger of the storm, she'd gone all the way back to the house. For him.

And now here he was in her penthouse apartment. In her world of wealth and privilege. Here he was...where he didn't belong.

Tit for tat.

That was true, because for a month of her life, Josie had existed in *his* world, where *she* didn't belong. And she'd done a helluva fine job of it. She'd even gotten her hands dirty by pulling weeds in his front yard. Oh, yeah, she was really something.

"Soup's on," Josie said, whizzing back into the room carrying a tray. She set it on the dresser, then planted her hands on her hips and looked at Max. "Okay, let's figure out how we're going to do this. If I put the pillows behind you, you ought to be sitting up enough to manage to eat."

"Whatever."

"Definitely grumpy."

Josie retrieved the pillow from the other side of the bed, then came back around to stand next to him. She leaned the pillow against the bed.

"Here's the plan," she said. "I'll help you sit up, then I'll fluff the pillow you're using, slide this other one into place and—ta-da—you'll be able to eat this outstanding meal."

Max nodded, propped his elbows firmly on the bed and attempted to push himself upward.

"Oh, Lord," he said with a groan. "My ribs."

Josie slid one arm behind Max's broad shoulders, then wrapped the other around his chest.

"Are you ready?" she said, turning her head to look at him.

"For what?" he said, gazing directly into her big, brown eyes.

Their lips were mere inches apart. The oh-so-familiar heat of desire rocketed through them, causing heartbeats to quicken and sensuous memories of lovemaking to flash in minds consumed by passion.

Max lifted one hand to the nape of Josie's neck and brought her mouth hard against his, delving his tongue between her lips.

Josie forgot everything and was aware only of the heated desire thrumming low and sweet in her body.

The kiss was heaven itself.

The kiss was Max.

A purr of pleasure whispered from her throat.

Josie, Max's mind hammered. It had been an eternity since he'd kissed her, tasted her, inhaled her aroma of sunshine and flowers. He wanted her. He burned for her. He was going up in flames of need.

Josie broke the kiss, lifting her head far enough to cause Max to drop his hand from her neck.

"Max, this is foolish," she said, her voice unsteady. "You're injured. We can't... What I mean is..."

"There are certain parts of my body that weren't hurt one bit by that damn tree."

"Yes, well... Come on. You really should eat. You must maintain your strength."

Max wiggled his eyebrows. "You betcha, babe. I

need every ounce of strength I can muster when you and I—''

''Hush. We're not discussing that.''

''But we will.''

''Hush.''

After a few fumbles with the pillow, accompanied by moans from Max, he was propped up, and the tray was set across his lap. He began to devour a huge ham sandwich and a bowl of fresh fruit.

''Not bad,'' he said between bites. ''How did you get a supply of food on hand so quickly? You haven't been home in a month.''

''There's a grocery story off the lobby downstairs. I just called in an order and they brought it up here.''

Max frowned. ''Easy living, huh? Snap your fingers and whatever you want is delivered.''

''Yes,'' Josie said, lifting her chin. ''That's how it works. Max, I'm not going to apologize for having money or for being a Wentworth. That's simply who I am. It doesn't mean that my life has automatically been bliss. Money can't erase the fact that my parents were killed when I was too young to remember them or what it felt like to be held in their arms, tucked into bed, hugged. And money can't erase that I just lost my beloved brother Jack. No amount of wealth or power is ever going to bring him back.''

''You're right,'' Max said quietly. ''I'm sorry, Josie. I was out of line.''

She nodded, then carried a desk chair from across the room and placed it next to the bed. She sat in it and looked at Max intently.

''I have to know, Max, I really do. Why? Why did

you hide my purse and my car? Why did you keep my identity from me?''

Max took the last bite of the meal, slid the tray onto the bed next to his legs, then sighed.

''At first I did it out of a sense of survival,'' he said. ''I was positive that your family, the mighty Wentworths, would sue me, take my ranch, because you'd been injured on my land. So I thought if I could just wait until your memory returned, we could sit down like sensible adults and agree that what had happened to you was an unfortunate accident. But then...''

''Then?'' Josie prompted, leaning slightly toward him.

''I hated the lies, Josie, I really did. I'd make up my mind to tell you the truth about who you were, then let the chips fall where they might. But I kept postponing the big confession because...because, hell, Josie, I didn't want you to leave the Single C, to leave me. Not yet.''

''I see.''

''What do you see? That I'm a liar? A rotten bum who—''

''No,'' she interrupted. ''I have a confession of my own. As my memory began to come back in bits and pieces, I remembered very early on that I'd had my purse with me that first day when I climbed onto the wagon with Rusty.''

''What?''

''I never told you that. I never asked you if we could go carefully over the route Rusty had taken so I could look for my purse.''

"Why didn't you?"

"Because what we were sharing was so special, so rare and wonderful. It was a fantasy world that I didn't want to end. Not yet. It all came crashing down on me when I found my purse in your closet.

"My first reaction, the one that sent me running from the house, was that you'd lied to me, betrayed me. I was shattered, so terribly hurt."

"Josie, I—"

"But now? Max, I lied to you, too, by keeping my silence about knowing I had that purse on the wagon. You have every right to be angry and hurt, too."

"Here we go again," he said, smiling slightly. "This isn't the first time we've both felt guilty about the same thing. Shall we handle it like we did before? Call a truce?"

"I'd like that," Josie said, smiling.

"Then consider it a done deal," Max said, matching her smile.

They continued to look directly into each other's eyes. Smiles faded as the embers of desire were fanned into licking flames once again. The air seemed to crackle with sensuality, like electrified threads weaving over and around them, pulling them closer and closer, although neither of them moved.

They were in their fantasy world, known only to them, created by and for only them. They weren't in a plush penthouse apartment with pristine white carpet, nor in a run-down ranch house with a muddy kitchen floor.

They were in *their* place, where passions soared,

wildflowers bloomed, and an amalgam of emotions tumbled one after the other.

"Oh, Max," Josie whispered, unable to tear her gaze from his.

"Josie," he returned, then cleared his throat when he heard the gritty sound of his voice. "What is this thing that happens between us? Beyond the desire, the want, what is this?"

He shook his head, breaking the spell, bringing them back to reality with a thud.

"Forget it," he said. "I don't want to know. I really don't."

Josie drew a much-needed breath, only then realizing she'd been hardly breathing while held mesmerized by Max's dark eyes.

"Why not?" she said. "Why don't you want to know what's happening between us?"

"What's the point?" Max frowned and swept one arm through the air. "Look at this room. I can only imagine what the rest of the place is like. This bedroom alone is bigger than my living room and kitchen put together. And white carpeting? White?"

Josie jumped to her feet. "And what, pray tell, is wrong with white carpeting? I happen to think it's very attractive. It creates an open, airy, floating-on-clouds atmosphere that I find soothing and peaceful."

"Oh, yeah? Well, I'll tell you what. I'll come tromping through your fancy-shmancy white-carpeted living room in my muddy boots, because that's who I am, a man with muddy boots and sweaty clothes. Maybe then you'll finally realize why there's no purpose to be served in wasting energy attempting to discover what's happening between us."

He paused. "Am I getting through to you? Our worlds don't mesh, Josie. Not even close. You belong here. I belong on the Single C. Do you understand what I'm saying, Josie *Wentworth?*"

"You betcha, babe. You're coming across loud and clear." She narrowed her eyes. "Well, get this, Carter. You're stuck here for now in this oh-so-awful world of large rooms and white carpeting, just as I was stuck on the Single C. Which is appropriately named, by the way. There isn't a woman born with a working brain who would be dumb enough to become seriously involved with such a narrow-minded grump of a man.

"But while you're in my home, buster, you'll be as pleasant as I was while in yours. I didn't even complain about your not having a dishwasher, for Pete's sake. So you'd better get your act together, Max Carter, because your ridiculous story about Granddad and me having a plan to starve you to death is beginning to hold a certain appeal. Got that?"

Josie spun on her heel and marched from the room.

A smile crept onto Max's lips. "You betcha, babe."

He dragged both hands down his face, erasing the smile in the process.

Why had he done that? Jumped all over Josie, been so nasty, rude and—okay—grumpy? Why? Because something major and important *was* growing between them. He'd lashed out at Josie because he'd had a rush of panic, of fear, that he just very might be falling in love with her.

No!

He wouldn't allow that. No way. He'd do his stint in her megabucks world, pay his debt of tit for tat, then he was going home to the Single C.

Where he belonged.

Alone.

Chapter Eleven

Max slept again, a deep, dreamless sleep that was disturbed by an unfamiliar voice calling, "Mr. Carter," and a firm grip shaking his shoulder.

He opened his eyes to find that night must have fallen, the only light in the bedroom from the glow of the lamp on the nightstand. He also found himself staring up at an enormous middle-aged woman in a white nurse's uniform.

"Well, it's about time you came around, Mr. Carter," she said. "I'm Gertie, your nurse."

"Huh?" Max frowned.

"Mr. Wentworth hired me to assist Ms. Wentworth with your care. We need to tend to nature's call, don't you think?"

"Huh?"

"Then we'll see about getting you some tasty

food. Ms. Wentworth has informed me that you haven't eaten anything for hours."

"Where *is* Josie?"

"She's in her library, I believe. Now then, dear boy, let's take care of necessary business, shall we?"

"Wait just a damn minute here," Max said none too quietly. "I don't need you to help me to... Go away and leave me alone."

"Fine," Gertie said, folding her arms across her ample bosom. "You just march yourself into the bathroom, and I'll wait right here for you."

"Oh, hell," Max muttered, dropping his chin to his chest.

"Exactly."

With the embarrassing-beyond-belief task having been attended to, Gertie produced a tray holding a hot, delicious offering of steak, mashed potatoes, vegetables and a big slice of cherry pie.

"Josie didn't make this," Max said, then shoveled in another forkful of potatoes. "It's terrific."

"Mr. Wentworth hired a cook for the duration of your recuperation here. He said he was aware of his granddaughter's, shall we say, limited abilities in the kitchen."

"Oh." Max nodded. "Is Josie, um, going to come in here and say hello to me?"

"I believe she said she had several weeks' worth of mail to sort through."

"What kind of mood is she in?"

"I really couldn't say, Mr. Carter," Gertie said, settling her large frame on the chair next to the bed. "Eat."

"Call me Max. It's a tad late to stand on formalities, considering what you...what we... Just call me Max."

"Fine. In the morning we're going to have a nice sponge bath and a shave."

"We are?" Max said, his eyebrows shooting up. "A sponge bath? No. Not a chance. There's no way in hell you're going to—"

"Yes, Max," Gertie said, a no-nonsense tone to her voice. "I am."

"Damn."

"Exactly."

The morning came and with it the promised sponge bath and shave, which Max did not suffer through quietly.

Gertie managed to change the sheets on the bed without causing him the least bit of physical discomfort, a process, Max had to admit, which was rather fascinating to watch. Gertie also produced a royal blue pajama top for him to wear.

After consuming an enormous breakfast, Max once again inquired about Josie's whereabouts.

"I saw her briefly," Gertie said. "She was heading back into her library." She set a stack of magazines next to Max on the bed. "Mr. Wentworth had these delivered for you this morning."

"I want to see Josie," Max said, glowering at Gertie.

"We're sounding like a pouty little boy. Why don't we read our magazines?"

"Because *we* don't want to," he said. "Go tell Josie that I want to see her. *Now.*"

"What's the magic word?"

"Oh, good Lord." Max shook his head. "This is a nightmare."

"Well?"

"Please!" he yelled.

"That's much better. I'll inquire as to whether Ms. Wentworth is available."

"You do that," Max said as Gertie bustled from the room.

Five minutes went by. Then ten.

Max's temper boiled hotter with every tick of the clock on the nightstand.

Fifteen minutes after Gertie had left the room, Josie appeared in the doorway, wearing winter white linen slacks and a mauve silk blouse.

"Where in hell have you been?" he roared.

"Goodbye, Max." Josie turned to leave.

"Wait, wait," he said quickly. "I'm sorry. I shouldn't have yelled. Okay? I'm sorry. But, cripes, Josie, you just disappeared and left me at the mercy of that amazon. Why did you do that?"

Josie walked forward slowly and sat down in the chair next to the bed.

"Because I'm tired of arguing with you, Max." There was no hint of a smile on her face. "I realize that you're in circumstances far from your liking, but every time we start a conversation, we end up screaming at each other. I've had enough of those upsetting scenes."

Max sighed. "Yeah, so have I. I apologize for being...so grumpy.'' He held out one hand toward her. ''Hey, I missed you. You look beautiful, by the way. Those clothes you're wearing are really nice. And that's not a slam dunk about how much they must have cost. It's a sincere compliment. You're a gorgeous woman, Ms. Wentworth.''

Josie dipped her head slightly and smiled. ''Thank you, Mr. Carter.'' She placed her hand in his where it rested palm up on the bed. ''How are you feeling this morning?''

''Not bad, all things considered.'' He chuckled. ''*We* had a bath and *we* had a shave and *we* tended to nature's call a couple of times. How about that? Hey, do you like my spiffy jammies?''

Josie laughed. ''They're stunning.''

''Someone ran off with the bottom half of them, though. I'm buck naked under this sheet.''

''Do tell.''

''Yep.''

''Well, pajama bottoms wouldn't fit over the cast on your leg, I guess. It's more efficient this way.''

''For all kinds of things,'' he said, grinning at her. ''*Very* efficient.''

''Don't start *that* again,'' she said, laughing.

Max's smile faded. ''I suppose your grandfather gave orders to someone to buy these pajamas, along with the magazines. And to hire Gertie and the cook. Why, Josie? Why is he doing all this?''

''I told you, I don't know. I still can't recall what I said to him at the ranch. I sure have spent a lot of time in the past weeks trying to drag information out of my poor brain.''

Max nodded. "Yeah, you have, and it's been rough on you. Maybe your grandfather will pop in here and explain his rationale."

"I doubt it. He seems determined that I figure this out on my own. Besides, he and my brother, Michael, have gone to Oklahoma City for a gathering of oil men."

"And left us unchaperoned?" Max said in mock horror. "What about my reputation? It'll be in shreds."

"Gertie is staying in the other guest room here, Mr. Carter."

"Oh. Well, cripes." Max paused. "Josie, I'd like to call Rusty sometime today to be certain that everything is under control at the Single C."

"Certainly. I'll plug a telephone into the jack in here. Feel free to call Rusty whenever you like. I know that the ranch is the most important thing in your life. You can't rest and recuperate properly if you're worried about what's going on there."

The ranch was the most important thing in his life? Max's mind echoed. Well, yes, of course, it was, always would be. Then again, that fact was just a tad difficult to remember when Josie Wentworth was within kissing distance of where he lay half-naked in bed.

"Do you want to play checkers?" Josie said.

"You own a game of checkers?"

"I do now. Granddad had a stack of games delivered. We have checkers, chess, Uno—even Candy Land and Chutes and Ladders."

"You're kidding," Max said, bursting into laughter.

"Be careful of your ribs, Max."

"They're coming along just fine. They were whacked worse than this when I was kicked by an ornery horse a few years ago."

"Does your leg hurt? Or your head?"

"My head's as good as new. My leg feels like a toothache. The cast sure is heavy, though."

"Well, Jeff said that once the bones start to heal, he'll change that cast for a lighter type—a walking cast."

"And I'll be able to go home." He rapped the bulky cast with his knuckles.

"Yes," Josie said quietly. "You'll be able to go home."

Max's head snapped around to meet Josie's gaze as he heard the soft, sad sound of her voice.

A cloud moved away from the sun, causing sunlight to pour through the window, falling over Josie like a golden waterfall. Max had a vivid image of that night weeks before when silvery moonlight had cascaded over her as she slept in the bed in the spare bedroom at the Single C.

Moonlight angel, he thought. That was what he'd called Josie in his mind that night. *His* moonlight angel. And they'd made love—exquisite love, like nothing he'd experienced before.

Now Josie was a sunshine angel, so lovely, so incredibly beautiful. And he wanted her even more than he had that night weeks ago.

"Max?" Josie said, her voice still hushed.

"What?" he said, pulling his mind back to attention.

"When you talk to Rusty, would you ask him to please have one of the workers my grandfather hired tend to the front yard of your house? Keep it free of weeds?"

"Yeah, sure." Max paused. "You actually care about that scruffy patch of dirt?"

"It is *not* scruffy, nor is it dirt. There was grass interspersed with those weeds—green, sweet grass. I put in a lot of hours shaping up that yard and, yes, I do care about it very much."

"Then I'll tell Rusty to make certain it gets put at the top of the chores list. I wonder what your grandfather would think if he knew you had done manual labor while you were at the Single C."

"He'd say that if it made me happy, then it's fine with him. Granddad has a reputation for being an honest but very shrewd and tough businessman, Max. He was a hard taskmaster about grades when Jack, Michael and I were in school, too. But there's also a softer side to him." She laughed. "He spoils me rotten. I'm his little Princess. If it makes me happy, then, by golly, I should have it."

Max smiled and nodded.

"I've been doing extensive volunteer work for several years," Josie went on. "That's not as lightweight as it may sound. I've developed organization, negotiation and accounting skills. I have a sharp eye for details, and I know how to delegate the right job to the best person. It's been very rewarding, but..." Her voice trailed off.

"But?" Max prompted.

"In the last letter I had from Jack, he urged me to start thinking of a career where I could apply those finely tuned skills."

"Sold," Max said. "Do you know how much paperwork is involved in running a ranch? It's grim, very grim. I hate it."

"There we go," Josie said, matching Max's lighthearted tone of voice. "I'll be the paperwork foreman of the Single C and you can punch the cows. How's that?" She frowned. "Do you actually punch your poor cows?"

Max chuckled. "They're cattle, not cows, and I wouldn't slug one of them on a bet, because I would probably get trampled into the ground and break my other leg. I have no idea where the term 'cowpuncher' came from."

"Interesting. I'll look it up on my computer."

"That's what I should do, you know. Have all the ranch records on computer. It sure would save me a hassle at tax-preparation time. I have to account for every head of cattle I own. They have numbered tags clipped to their ears. The calves have to be branded, tagged, recorded... Man, I'm getting a headache just thinking about it. My records are sloppy at best."

"Fear not," Josie said, raising one finger in the air. "The new firm of Josie Wentworth, Ranch Manager—which is all of five minutes old—will make order out of your terrible chaos, sir."

"Well, I'll rest easier here in my white-carpeted prison now that I know that, ma'am."

They smiled at each other, both thoroughly enjoying the comfortable ease of their conversation.

But then, echoes of what they'd said crept into their minds at the same time, causing smiles to fade and frowns to materialize, as they continued to gaze directly into each other's eyes.

A career where I can apply my finely tuned skills.

Sold.

I'll be the paperwork manager of the Single C, and you can punch the cows.

Order out of your terrible chaos, sir.

I'll rest easier now that I know that, ma'am.

Josie tore her gaze from Max's. "Well," she said, getting to her feet. "I should let you get some rest."

"Yeah, I'm tired, which is ridiculous, seeing as how I'm not doing anything except lying here like a slug."

"Your body has suffered a tremendous trauma, Max. You definitely need your rest. I'll see you later. Bye."

Josie hurried from the room, not stopping until she reached the leather chair behind the desk in her library. Sitting down, she pressed trembling hands to her flushed cheeks.

Josie, get a grip, she told herself. She and Max had just been chatting, being silly, engaging in a nonsensical conversation to pass the time.

She wasn't really going to embark on a career of ranch management. To be more precise, she wasn't going to manage that portion of the running of the Single C. Working side by side. As Max's partner.

Doing her part, while he did his to make a success of the ranch. As Max's lover.

As Max's wife.

"Stop it," she whispered.

She and Max had been fooling around. He'd no doubt already forgotten what their idle chitchat had been about.

Her damnable imagination was running roughshod over reality. She'd do well to remember the name of Max's ranch.

The *Single* C.

Max stared at the doorway Josie had disappeared through, willing his thundering heart to quiet its wild tempo.

For a moment, while he'd been gazing into Josie's eyes, it had all seemed possible, within his reach, his to have. Josie. His wife. His life's partner, his work partner on the ranch, the mother of his children.

Just for a moment it had been real.

Was that what he really wanted? he wondered, feeling beads of sweat dot his brow. Deep within the very essence of himself was he lonely?

He swiped the sweat away, then dragged his hands down his face.

Was he lonely? his mind repeated. Why didn't he know? Shouldn't that be a question that was easily answered? Or was a part of him refusing to address it because he knew that Josie Wentworth was not his to have?

Was he falling in love with her? Was he already in love with her? *Damn it, he didn't know.*

* * *

The next week, by unspoken agreement, neither Josie nor Max broached any serious subjects during their chats or while playing board games together.

A wheelchair had been delivered to Josie's apartment, presumably ordered by Joseph. The chair had one straight panel where Max could rest his cast. Gertie covered his lower body with a blanket, preserving his modesty.

To his own amazement, Max had not been overwhelmed by the opulence of Josie's apartment the first time she pushed his chair through the rooms for a tour.

He complimented her sincerely on her home, her taste in decorating, accepting what he saw as a reflection of who she was.

The view from the tall, gleaming windows was breathtaking, and Max lost track of time as he gazed out over the city. He blanked his mind and allowed a sense of peace and tranquillity to flow through him.

He couldn't remember when he'd sat so still for so long. He was accustomed to working long hours on the ranch, tending to the never-ending chores.

But he'd vowed that he would adjust to Josie's world as well as she had to his, and by damn, he was doing it.

The days in the penthouse fell into a comfortable routine, just as they had on the Single C. Max spoke on the telephone to Rusty each morning and was told daily that all was well at the ranch. The men Joseph Wentworth had hired were working fools, the old cowboy had cackled, and the spread had never looked so good.

Early in the morning on the tenth day since Max had taken up residency in her apartment, Josie entered her library and closed the door. She needed some quiet time, some private time, before she greeted Max with her usual smile and cheery hello.

Moving behind the desk, she sat down in the leather chair slowly and carefully, feeling suddenly fragile, as though she might shatter like delicate china.

She'd been living in a fantasy world again, just as she had at the Single C. This time the glorious ball was being held at *her* home. The prince had come to *her*. But there was a clock hovering in the shadows of the penthouse, just as there'd been for the Cinderella who'd resided at the ranch.

Tick...tick...tick.

The glorious days with Max were passing so quickly. Even though they stayed clear of serious matters, didn't discuss again Josie's silly proposal of becoming a ranch manager, didn't delve one inch into Max's protected past, they never ran out of things to talk about.

Each night when she kissed Max good night before going to her own room, desire flared instantly—hot, swirling, consuming. They would break the heated kiss reluctantly, and she would go quickly to her own bed—her big, lonely bed.

Tick...tick...tick.

Josie closed her eyes, gathering courage, forcing

herself to snap out of the wondrous make-believe world with Max and stand firmly in reality.

She opened her eyes, looked at the calendar on the desk, then pressed one hand against her flat stomach.

The time had come.

She had to know.

Was she pregnant with Max Carter's baby?

Tick…tick…tick.

With a trembling hand, she flipped through the pages of her address book until she found the name of her doctor.

Then, as though watching herself from afar, she saw her hand float upward and lift the receiver to the telephone.

Tick…tick…tick…

Chapter Twelve

Late that afternoon Josie stood in front of a department-store window, giving the impression, she hoped, that she was totally engrossed in the expensive clothes on the mannequins.

In actuality, because of the way the sun was striking the glass, she was able to see her own reflection as clearly as if she was staring into a mirror.

She stood statue-still, hardly breathing, searching for something, anything, that was visual evidence of the difference between the Josie Wentworth who'd left her apartment several hours before and who she was now.

She looked exactly the same, she thought in amazement. That hardly seemed possible, considering that her life—her entire future—had just been turned upside down.

"Oh, isn't that gorgeous?" a woman said.

Josie jerked in surprise at the sudden intrusion into her thoughts.

"What?" she said, turning her head toward the woman now standing next to her.

"That black dress. The one in the middle there. Isn't it beautiful?"

"Oh, yes, it certainly is," Josie said, looking at the creation for the first time. "It's very elegant, simple but classy."

The woman sighed. "And I'd never go anywhere to wear it. When you have three little kids, you're lucky to get out to a movie once in a while." She laughed. "If my husband and I went out to dinner, I'd probably get up and start clearing the table. Oh, well, so it goes. I wouldn't trade my babies for all the fancy nights on the town in the world."

"No, of course you wouldn't," Josie said.

"Do you have children?" the woman asked pleasantly.

Josie drew a steadying breath. "I just came from the doctor's office, where I was told that I'm pregnant. I'm...I'm going to have a baby." She smiled. "There. I said it right out loud for the first time. It's really sinking in. It's true. I'm going to have a beautiful, healthy, wonderful baby."

The woman beamed. "Well, bless your heart. Congratulations. You're obviously thrilled, so I assume your husband will be, too. Oh, look at the time. I must dash. Every happiness to you and your husband. What a lucky little baby to have parents so excited about its arrival. Bye."

"Goodbye," Josie said, then turned and walked slowly down the sidewalk.

So much for euphoria, she thought. That conversation had brought her back to reality with a jarring thud, to say the least.

She didn't have a husband, let alone one who would be thrilled upon hearing her news. The last thing Max Carter, of the Single C Ranch, wanted in his life was a wife and baby.

Josie crossed the street and entered a small park, pulling her coat closer around her as she settled onto a bench beneath a tree. A chilly breeze whispered by, and she shivered.

She'd gotten pregnant the very first time she and Max had made love, she was certain, when birth control had been the farthest thing from their minds.

Oh, how cocky they'd been, feeling so in charge, so in control of their lives in their world beyond reality. The rancher and the woman with no memory, pretending that everything was perfect as they meshed their bodies night after night, ignoring the fact that they weren't one entity in heart and soul.

"What are you going to do, Josie Wentworth?" she murmured as she watched a pigeon waddle past. "This is reality-check time, remember?"

She was Josie Wentworth, of the famous Wentworth Oil Works family of Oklahoma, a family who made tabloid news if they so much as sneezed twice in a row.

She was twenty-nine years old, single and carrying the baby of a man who was land-poor.

A man who refused to share his innermost thoughts and dreams with her.

A man who moved through life alone and fully intended to continue to do so.

A man…

Josie stiffened and her breath caught. Out of nowhere, as vividly as though she was living it at that very moment, she saw in her mind's eye the scene in Max's kitchen when she'd run through the door seeking help for him. She was clutching her grandfather's suit jacket as she sobbed out her heartfelt plea.

Oh, Granddad, please, you've got to help Max. He came looking for me because I… It's all my fault that he's hurt and…a tree in the woods…the lightning… Granddad, please, Max is pinned beneath a tree. He's unconscious, but he's alive, and I promised him I'd get help for him. Please, Granddad, please. I love him. He's my Max. Please, you've got to—

I love him.

He's my Max.

I love him…I love him…I love him…

"Oh, dear heaven," Josie whispered as the words echoed over and over in her mind.

And her heart.

And her soul.

She was in love with Max Carter.

Yes. Yes, she was. She knew that now, knew she'd buried that staggering fact deep within her, knew there was no longer anywhere to hide from the truth.

That was what Joseph Wentworth was waiting for her to remember.

That was why he'd moved heaven and earth to place Max securely in her apartment.

He knew she was in love with Max Carter, and anything his precious Princess wanted, by damn, she would have.

"Not this time, Granddad," Josie said, her eyes misting with tears.

Max Carter couldn't be bought. The Wentworth power and money meant nothing. Max's love didn't have a price tag on it that could be met easily by a snap of mighty Wentworth fingers.

Josie sighed, then dashed away the tears that slid down her cheeks.

She was in love for the first time in her life. Deeply, irrevocably in love. But the man of her heart didn't love her, didn't want her as his life partner, his wife, nor would he want their baby, who was nestled deep within her.

"Oh, God," she said, a sob in her voice, "what am I going to do?"

No, no, no! she told herself in the next instant. She was not going to fall apart, dissolve into a weeping mess of despair. Absolutely not.

She lifted her chin and swallowed past the ache of unshed tears in her throat.

She was a Wentworth.

She was strong, stood tall in the face of adversity.

She wanted this baby, would rejoice in this child, raise it with heartfelt love—alone.

She'd survive the hateful glee of reporters splashing stories across the tabloids about one of the oh-so-proper and important Wentworths stepping over the line of convention and becoming an unwed mother.

Josie Wentworth To Have Love Child, the headlines would probably scream. So be it. Let them do their worst, she didn't care. Love child? Fine. Yes. She would love this child and its father until the day she died.

She would ask nothing of Max, wouldn't attempt to force him into a life he wanted no part of.

Should she even tell Max about the baby? Did a man have a right—no matter what his reaction to the news might be—to know he was going to be a father?

Yes, she supposed he did. She would tell Max about their child when the time was right, when her courage about facing the future alone was more firmly grounded. He would be told—but not yet.

Josie got to her feet and walked slowly along the cobbled sidewalk in the park.

She wasn't ready to go home, she realized. She needed some space, some solitude, to come to grips with the newly discovered truth of her love for Max Carter and with the existence of their baby.

At the edge of the park Josie stopped at a public telephone, dropped change into the slot and pressed the buttons of her number at the apartment, ignoring the visible trembling of her hand. The telephone was answered on the second ring.

"Wentworth residence."

"Gertie? This is Josie. May I speak with Max, please, if he's awake?"

"Of course, Ms. Wentworth. Max is reading a novel while sitting in his favorite place in front of the windows. He does enjoy that spectacular view."

"Yes, he does," Josie said. And she would envision him there long after he'd returned to the Single C, long after he'd left her—forever. "Wold you give him the portable phone, please?"

"Certainly," Gertie said.

One second, two, then three went by, with Josie's heartbeat increasing with each one.

"Josie?"

"Hi, Max," she said, forcing a lightness to her voice. "Listen, I won't be home for dinner. In fact, it may be quite late before I get back."

"Is something wrong?"

"No, no, not really. I bumped into the woman who took over the volunteer project I was in charge of. She stepped in for me when I attempted to find your cousin Sabrina.

"Anyway, as the new chairperson, she's running into difficulties with some of the details. I'm going to sit down with her and go over everything. It's the least I can do, considering I dumped the whole business on her with no notice. I really feel I should come to her rescue a bit here.

"So you see, I don't know what time I'll be home. I don't want you to be concerned. I mean, I have a reputation for bumping my head, getting amnesia and disappearing without a trace."

"So you do. I appreciate the call, Josie. I would've been worried when you didn't show up for dinner."

"There. I knew it. So I called. Yes, I certainly did. Well, I must go. I'll talk to you...whenever. Okay? Bye."

Josie replaced the receiver quickly and drew a much-needed breath.

She was such a lousy liar, she thought with self-disgust. She always chattered like a magpie when she wasn't telling the truth. Well, Max hadn't known she'd been fibbing. He'd accepted her excuse without question.

Max didn't realize that she'd lied.

Josie was lying, Max thought, staring at the portable telephone, a frown knitting his dark brows. She'd been talking so fast it was a wonder she hadn't passed out from lack of oxygen.

What in the hell was going on? What was Josie really up to? She hadn't sounded upset, but how could he have determined if she actually was since she'd babbled in his ear?

"Damn it," Max said, glaring at the bulky cast on his leg.

He was helpless, had no choice but to sit there in his fancy wheelchair and wait.

Wait for Josie to come home.

To him.

Max swept his troubled gaze over the spacious, white-carpeted living room.

Home, he mentally repeated. It was amazing that he'd become so comfortable in a place so foreign to what he was accustomed to, just as Josie had at the Single C. Well, he'd made up his mind that he could do it, and he had.

But...

Was he relaxed and at peace in a plush penthouse apartment due to his own determination to "go with the flow"? Or was it because the days spent here were with Josie?

Good question, he thought dryly, but he didn't know the answer. Besides, the issue at hand was Josie, and why she was out there somewhere, staying away from the apartment, from him.

Max turned to stare out the window.

What's wrong, Josie? What's going on in that beautiful, complicated, fascinating mind of yours? Please, Josie, come home and talk to me.

What Josie is doing is none of your business, Carter, a little voice rasped in his brain.

He had a hard-line stand on not invading another's privacy, had hollered that at Josie when she'd first arrived at the ranch in search of Sabrina.

He'd held fast to that principle, refusing to share any of his history, his past, with Josie, keeping all conversations skimming on the surface, allowing no depth, no real sharing of his inner secrets, hopes or dreams.

But now? Damn, the tables had been turned on him. Josie was out there somewhere, dealing with personal and private things, had kept him at arm's length by lying about where she was going and why.

And it hurt.

There was an actual, physical pain slicing through his gut, slamming against his heart.

Tit for tat.

Josie was dishing out exactly what he'd been serving up to her since the very first day they'd met. She was suddenly operating by his etched-in-stone code of conduct.

He felt isolated and lonely, shut out, cut off from a part of Josie she was now refusing to share with him.

Max drew a deep, shuddering breath, then let it out slowly.

He was a simple man, a rancher, a rough-edged, earthy cowboy in sweaty, dirty clothes, the result of honest labor on the land he loved.

He worked, ate, slept, then started all over again the next day with the same program. That was who he was, who he'd been all of his adult life.

But it wasn't enough, not now. Not since Josie had entered his narrow existence and filled it to overflowing. He wanted more. Dear Lord, he *needed* more.

He needed Josie.

"Man, oh, man," Max said, dragging his hands down his face.

He had changed so much, been given a glimpse of a whole new, wonderful world since the day Josie had arrived at the ranch and he'd stood so arrogantly in charge, in control, delivering his sermons to her on the subject of personal privacy.

He'd come to anticipate entering his shabby little house at day's end, because he knew that Josie would be there, smiling, welcoming him into her soft, feminine embrace, having prepared an endearingly, hardly edible dinner for them.

He'd learned to really listen to what Josie said to him as they chatted through the evening hours. He savored the sound of her voice, her delicate wind-chime laughter, felt heated desire zing through him when she smiled at him, saw mirrored in her captivating eyes the building passion that was being fanned once more from glowing embers into licking flames.

Desire. Never fully quelled, it simmered, waiting for the moment when he and Josie would again mesh their bodies, become one entity, while sharing love-making so exquisitely beautiful it was beyond description.

His bed, with its saggy mattress and faded, worn sheets, was no longer just a platform to drop onto in total exhaustion from pushing his stamina to the maximum and more, as he tended to the never-ending chores on the ranch.

That bed was now a haven of awe and wonder, encased in a mystical haze of sensual beauty and fulfillment.

That bed was going to be so damn big and empty when he returned to the Single C. When he went back where he belonged. Alone. Without Josie. Forever.

"No," Max said, his voice a hoarse whisper.

He would not—*could not*—face a future without Josie. A future so empty, cold and lonely.

No, that wasn't acceptable, and it was *not* going to happen because...

Max stiffened in the wheelchair, every muscle in his body tensing to the point that a searing pain shot through his injured leg.

Because he...ah, damn it, he was in love with Josie Wentworth.

"Carter, you idiot," he said, slamming a fist on the arm of the chair. "You stupid fool."

He'd done it, he thought with self-directed fury. He'd actually gone and fallen in love with Josie. Ms. Josie Wentworth, of the Wentworth Oil Works family. The rich and powerful Wentworths. Josie, who lived in a penthouse apartment with white carpeting.

I'll be the paperwork manager of the Single C and you can punch the cows.

Order out of your terrible chaos, sir.

I'll rest easier now that I know that, ma'am.

"Yeah, right," Max said, a bitter edge to his voice.

Those words had been spoken during a conversation of silly playfulness. Josie wasn't about to take up a career of ranch management.

To manage a ranch—his ranch—Josie would have to live there, be his partner in business, his soul mate in life.

His wife.

The mother of his children.

Josie would have to walk away from a world of wealth, social status, a place where the mere announcement of her last name brought people to saluting attention, eager to do her bidding.

She would have to be so in love with him, land-poor Max Carter, that she'd be willing to turn her back on a life-style he could never match, never offer her. A life-style that was rightfully hers to have.

And that just wasn't going to happen. None of it. Not ever.

The only saving grace to the whole scenario was that at least he would leave here, return to where he belonged with his pride intact, with Josie having no clue as to his true emotions.

He continued to stare out the window, no longer seeing the awe-inspiring view displayed before him.

He saw only a bleak and empty future stretching into the lonely eternity that would be the remainder of his days—and nights.

He saw only a world of dark clouds and shadows, because his moonlight and sunshine angel would be not be standing by his side.

Time lost meaning as Max sat in the wheelchair in the huge quiet room, sinking deeper into a black pit of despair.

He simply sat there, waiting for Josie to come home.

Josie ordered a dinner she didn't want in a small, cozy restaurant. She forced herself to blank her mind, to take a mental reprieve from thoughts of the tangled mess of her life.

She ate every morsel of food on her plate, having to nearly choke it down, knowing she was consuming the nutritious meal for the precious baby, the miracle, tucked deep within her.

After leaving the restaurant, she drove to a mall

that had a movie theater, bought a ticket and dropped into a seat in the back row.

She was still postponing going home, she knew. She just didn't want to see Max, talk to Max, not yet.

The movie started with a blast of noise and vivid colors, but Josie tuned it out, turning inward to the essence of herself, reaching for the strength and courage she would need in the days, weeks and years to come.

And slowly it came, filling her, bringing with it a modicum of peace that helped soothe the pain that came with the realization that she was in love with a man who didn't love her, a man whose baby she was carrying.

She allowed cleansing tears to slide freely down her cheeks as she sat unnoticed in the dark theater.

When the movie ended, she got to her feet and walked out into the night, knowing it was time to go home.

Just before midnight Josie closed the apartment door with a quiet click and saw that a lamp had been left on for her in the living room. She moved forward, dropped her purse on the sofa, slipped off her shoes, then swept her gaze over the room.

It was so big, so empty-looking, she thought. So silent. She wouldn't live here after the baby was born. She wanted a house with a yard where a child could play. Plus, there were too many haunting memories of Max within these walls.

And besides, she thought with a smile, she'd have

to be crazy to raise a busy little one in a home with white carpeting.

As she started toward the hallway, her destination the safe haven of her bedroom, she stopped, frowning as a strange sensation suffused her.

It was as though she was being pulled by a gently tugging, silken thread that urged her to change her course.

Her heartbeat quickened and heat began to thrum hot and low within her.

Max.

Of their own volition, it seemed, her feet moved her from the plush carpeting in the living room, down the hall and into Max's bedroom.

She stood next to his bed, listening to the rhythm of his breathing as he slept, just barely able to see his silhouette in the dim slivers of light that reached from the lamp in the living room.

As her eyes adjusted to the near darkness, she saw him more clearly, savoring the sight of his rugged features, his thick, tousled hair.

He'd removed the pajama top for the night and his bare chest beckoned her to entwine her fingers in the dark, curling hair.

I'm home, Max, Josie whispered in her mind. *I'm here, my love, and I want you, need you. I love you, Max Carter. I love you and our baby, and I will for all time.*

Josie crossed the room, closed and locked the door, then shed her clothes, dropping them on the floor. She returned to the other side of the bed and slipped beneath the sheet and blanket.

She nestled as close to Max as the bulky cast would allow, then eased upward carefully to kiss his slightly parted lips.

"Mmm," Max murmured in his sleep.

Josie kissed him again, her tongue stroking his in the darkness of his mouth.

Max's eyes flew open and in the next instant he cradled Josie's head in his large hands, urging her mouth harder onto his as he responded to her kiss with rough urgency. When his breathing became labored, he broke the kiss, raising Josie's head a fraction of an inch.

"Josie," he said, his voice gritty with passion. "You're home."

"Yes, Max, I'm home," she whispered.

"Are you all right? On the phone you sounded...I don't know...you were—"

"Shh. All that matters is that we're together and I want to make love with you, but your ribs—"

"Hey, don't worry about them. I'm burning for you, Josie."

"Oh, Max, I... No, we won't talk anymore, not now. All right?"

"You betcha, babe," Max said, then claimed her lips in a searing kiss.

This, Max thought hazily, *is the woman I love, the only woman I have ever, will ever, love. This is Josie. She came home...to me, and for now she's mine.*

Max lifted Josie up and over the cast, never breaking the kiss as he settled her on top of his heated body.

I'm making love, Josie thought, *with the father of*

my child. I am making love with the man who has stolen my heart forever. Tonight is ours. Tonight he's mine.

Max splayed his hands on Josie's smooth back, then skimmed them lower to cup the feminine roundness of her buttocks. His arousal was heavy, aching with want.

"Josie," he said, close to her lips, "it's been so long. I want you so damn much."

"Yes."

Max gripped her waist as she shifted upward, then he lifted her onto him, filling her with all that he was, all that he had to give.

Josie received him, glorying in the sensual ecstasy he brought to her. She straddled him, taking care not to bump his injured leg.

And then the dance began, with Josie setting the tempo, rising, falling, moving to music only they could hear. They danced on, faster now, harder, wanting it all, wanting to burst onto the exquisite place that was theirs to share together.

"Ah, Josie," Max said, lifting his hips with a groan of male pleasure as he found his release.

"Max!"

Josie flung back her head, savoring every second of the mystical haze Max had taken her to, then she collapsed against him.

"Oh, Max," she said, her voice ringing with awe. She paused. "Your ribs. I—"

"Don't move. You feel wonderful right where you are. Don't go."

"No, I won't leave you, Max. Not yet."

"No," he said quietly, "not yet."

Chapter Thirteen

Max slept late the next morning, waking finally to the aroma of cooking bacon wafting through the air—and the sight of Jeff Wilson sitting in the chair next to the bed.

"What..." Max started, then glanced quickly at the rumpled sheets on the other side of the bed that were the only evidence Josie had been there. He looked at Jeff again. "What are you doing here?"

"Turning green with envy at the quality of your recuperation accommodations," Jeff said, smiling.

"Yeah, well, it's been hard to take," Max said, sliding both hands beneath his head on the pillow. "But I'm tough, brave and bold. I just gritted my teeth and put up with it all. You know what I mean?"

"I know you're full of bull, Carter." Jeff laughed and shook his head. "I've never even stayed in a hotel this fancy. A penthouse apartment? Whew. You're one lucky cowboy."

"Right." Max frowned and pulled his hands free. "This *lucky* cowboy has a busted leg."

"Which brings us back to your question of what I'm doing here."

"Oh?"

"I showed your X rays to a specialist yesterday, and he agreed with me that the cast put on that leg was a bit of overkill. I'm not saying it wasn't a bad break, but..."

"But?"

"The damage is below your knee. If you took it easy, used common sense and didn't stay on your feet too long at a stretch, you could make do with a walking cast."

"A walking cast," Max repeated, his frown deepening. "That would make it possible for me to—" a sudden and unexpected chill swept through him "—leave here and go back to the ranch."

"Yep. I had strict instructions from Joseph Wentworth to keep him fully informed of your progress. I called him yesterday afternoon, brought him up-to-date, and he had me flown in a private plane here to Freemont Springs bright and early this morning.

"There's an ambulance down at the curb waiting to take us to the hospital to change that cast, then we're flying home."

"Today?" Max raised himself up on his elbows. "Don't I have any say in this? Damn it, Jeff, it's *my* leg."

"You're a rancher, not a doctor. You don't get to

vote. As soon as you've had some breakfast, we're out of here." Jeff got to his feet. "I'm going to go have a second breakfast. Some of us have been up for hours, unlike someone else. Oh, and shave before we leave, would you? You look like crud."

"But..." Max sank back onto the pillow as Jeff left the room. "Hell."

He was leaving today? Leaving Josie in just a couple of hours? His mind raced. No! It wasn't supposed to happen yet. *Damn it, not yet.*

Josie had come to him last night, sweet and loving, wanting him as much as he wanted her. He still didn't know where she'd been until so late or why. All he knew was that she'd come home to *him* and they'd made love—beautiful, wonderful love.

Max dragged both hands down his face.

Josie. The woman he loved, the only woman he'd ever loved. No, he couldn't leave her. He'd tell her to pack a suitcase because he was taking her home, with him, where she belonged. They'd be married and have four kids—hell, they'd have six kids. They'd laugh and love and be so damn happy. Josie...

"Wentworth," Max said dismally.

No, Josie wasn't going home with him. She would stay right here in her world, with its penthouse apartment, white carpeting and all the other fancy trimmings her money could buy.

Josie cared for him, he knew she did. But even if she was in love with him—which he seriously doubted—she'd never consent to living on the Single

C, making do with the little he could offer her. It wouldn't be enough. *He* wouldn't be enough.

The Single C. Man, he could remember the day he'd registered that name and the brand he'd be using on his cattle. He'd been so smug, cocky, silently laughing at the way he was declaring loud and clear that Max Carter didn't need anyone in his life.

The Single C. That logo would haunt him now, taunt him with its empty sound, echo in his mind like painful, physical blows. It would shout the fact day in, day out, and through the endless stretch of nights that lay before him, that he was, indeed, single. Alone. Lonely. Because Josie wouldn't be by his side.

"Max?"

He looked up quickly to see Josie coming toward him slowly, carrying a tray.

Ah, look at her, Max thought. There she was. His incredible Josie. The woman of his heart, his mind, his soul. The woman he loved. The woman he was about to leave—forever.

"I...I have your breakfast," she said, stopping next to the bed.

"Oh, yeah, sure, okay. Thank you."

Max fumbled with the pillows, pushed himself up, then took the tray from her. She sat down in the chair and clutched her hands tightly together in her lap.

"You're awfully pale, Josie," he said, then picked up a fork. "Are you all right?"

All right? Josie thought. No, she wasn't remotely close to being all right. She'd had a bout of morning sickness that had left her weak and trembling.

Then an hour after that she'd opened the door to a smiling Jeff Wilson, who had breezily announced he was getting that lazy lout Max Carter out of her way today, and wasn't it about time?

She'd wanted to shove Jeff back into the hallway, slam the door on him and the words he'd spoken, make the cold, stark reality disappear.

Dear God, Max was leaving her today.

Her beloved Max, the father of the baby who'd definitely made its presence known as she'd dashed for the bathroom at dawn.

Max, the man she loved so much, so very much, was going to be whisked away in a handful of minutes.

Tick...tick...tick.

No. Please, no. Not yet. Not yet.

"Josie?" Max said, concern etched on his face as he looked at her.

"What? Oh. I...I'm fine, Max. I'm just...well, rather stunned at this sudden change in plans. You know, Jeff arriving and saying you're going to get a walking cast and then return to the ranch and..."

Tears filled her eyes.

"I'm...you're... Dear heaven, Max, you're leaving." She waved one hand in the air. "Ignore me. I just hate goodbyes of any kind. We knew this day would come."

"But not yet," Max said quietly.

"No." Josie swept the tears away as they spilled onto her cheeks. "Not yet."

Max nodded, poked at the eggs on the plate with the fork, then set the tray next to him on the bed.

"Is something wrong with the food?" Josie asked.

"I've lost my appetite. Josie, listen, I want you to know that if I hear from my cousin Sabrina, I'll tell her you'd like to speak with her about your brother Jack. I'll give her your address and telephone number."

"But—"

"I know, I know," he said, raising one hand. "I had an unbendable stand on the issue of personal privacy, but...well, let's just say I've changed my stubborn mind-set."

"You have?" Josie said, straightening a bit in the chair.

"Josie, you made me realize that it's not a clear-cut, black-and-white issue. There are times when caring and sharing are needed."

"Oh," she said, feeling the tempo of her heart increase.

"I understand now," Max went on, "why you read the letter addressed to Sabrina and why you came to the ranch hoping to find her. I'm sorry I was so hard on you about that. Will you accept my apology?"

"Yes. Yes, of course, I will," she said, fighting against more threatening tears.

Oh, Max, she thought. How difficult it must have been for a man like him to have said those words. Accept his apology? She'd wrap it up like a precious gift and hug it close to her heart.

Max had changed. But how much and in what other ways? Would he now trust her enough to reveal more of his past and his dreams for the future? Did the importance of caring and sharing extend to him, as well as her search for Sabrina?

She'd have to move slowly, and so very carefully, to discover just how far-reaching the changes to Max Carter went.

But...

Tick...tick...tick.

There wasn't time!

The clock was going to strike at any moment. As soon as Jeff finished eating his breakfast, Max would be bundled up and taken away, torn from her embrace.

No! It wasn't fair. They couldn't be separated now. Not now. Not yet. Fate was pointing a stern finger, ordering Max to return to his world and her to remain where she was.

Dear heaven, what should she do?

The changes in Max, what they might mean to her, to them, were too fragile, too new, for her to announce that she was packing a suitcase and going with him. She didn't even know if he truly wanted her to remain by his side.

And what about the baby?

She couldn't tell Max about their child now, then have Jeff walk into the room in the next second.

Tick...tick...tick.

"Are we finished with our breakfast?" Gertie said, bustling into the room. "What's this? We haven't eaten hardly a bite?"

"*We* aren't hungry," Max said, glaring at her.

"Well, we'll be a hungry boy by lunch hour,

won't we? So be it. Shall we have a wash and a shave?"

Josie got to her feet. "I'll get out of your way so you can tend to...things."

"Josie—" Max began.

"Excuse me," she said, then hurried from the room.

When Josie rushed into the living room, she nearly bumped into her grandfather, who was standing just beyond the hallway.

"Granddad," she said, her eyes widening in surprise. "What are you doing here?"

"I'm just making certain that everything goes smoothly, that my orders are carried out as I directed. Max is still recuperating. I don't want him worn to a frazzle by any slipups."

"That's very considerate of you," she said, sinking onto a chair. "Max will be all set to go shortly. He'll be ready...to leave. To go home. To his ranch. Where...where he belongs and...and wants to be."

"Is something wrong, Princess?" Joseph said, raising his eyebrows.

Josie narrowed her eyes and looked up at her grandfather. He was waiting for her to say she had remembered sobbing out her declaration of love for Max that day in Max's kitchen.

The innocent expression on Joseph Wentworth's face was a bunch of baloney.

Well, nice try, Granddad, but no cigar.

She wasn't about to start weeping on mighty Joseph Wentworth's shirtfront about how much she loved Max. Why was her granddad so determined to ship Max home so quickly, with no notice, no warning?

She wasn't going to make that kind of a spectacle of herself when she didn't know the depths of Max Carter's feelings for her.

"Wrong?" she said, forcing herself to smile pleasantly. "No, nothing is wrong. This is just a rather chaotic start to my day. All this hubbub has jangled my nerves."

Don't say another word, Josie Wentworth, she ordered herself. For once in her life she wasn't going to babble like an idiot while she was lying through her teeth. For the first time in her twenty-nine years on this earth, she was going to get a bold-faced lie past her granddad.

Joseph leaned slightly toward her. "You're positive nothing is upsetting you—beyond your jangled nerves from all this activity?"

Josie executed a huge yawn, patting her hand against her open mouth.

"I'm sleepy," she said when her performance was completed. "I was out late last night. Once everyone's out of here, I'm going to take a nap."

"You were out late?" Joseph said, his voice rising. "You just waltzed yourself out the door to do the town, leaving Max alone to stare at the walls while trapped in his wheelchair?"

"Granddad, I'm not his baby-sitter. How many games of Candy Land can a person play before going nuts?"

"I did something wrong while raising you, young

lady. Your going out last night was a selfish thing to do."

Josie shrugged. "Whatever. I certainly had a good time, though."

"I need a cup of coffee," Joseph said, then strode from the room.

She'd done it, Josie mentally cheered. She'd pulled it off with Academy Award-winning skill. All she had to do now was keep from dissolving into a sobbing mess on the floor when she watched Max being taken out of the apartment.

All she had to do was witness Max Carter leaving her—forever.

Josie closed her eyes and pressed both hands to her stomach, envisioning the baby growing there.

She had to hang on, she thought. Be strong. Be a Wentworth. She could do it. She had to. She'd figure out later how to inform Max about their child.

But when the door to her big, empty apartment closed behind Max Carter, she was going to cry, and cry and cry.

In the kitchen Joseph nodded absently to the cook, who announced that she was leaving since her assignment was completed. When the woman was gone, Joseph sat down opposite Jeff at the table.

"This isn't going well, Wilson," Joseph said, frowning, his voice hushed.

"Let's give Josie and Max some time to allow the fact that they're about to be separated to really sink in," Jeff said, keeping his voice low. "They were both surprised by my news, you know. Stunned."

"Hmm," Joseph said, his frown deepening. "Josie is acting as though she'll be glad to have everyone out of here so she can take a nap, for heaven's sake. I swear, that girl is so stubborn."

"I wonder who she takes after?" Jeff said, smiling.

"Yes, yes, I know," Joseph said impatiently. "She reminds me of myself when she lifts that chin and pokes her nose in the air. There's no budging her. But, damn it, Jeff, I know she loves Max Carter. She said it herself that day he got hurt."

"She *was* awfully upset, though."

"Which is even better. Those words just spilled out, without her thinking. Oh, she's in love with Carter, all right. She doesn't remember telling me that she is, but I know it's true."

"My wife and I agree with you," Jeff said. "We saw Josie and Max together. I'd never seen Max act like he had with her. He was so open, so at ease, so happy. But I have to tell you that if you're running a stubborn contest, Max would win hands down."

"Damn it," Joseph said, smacking the top of the table with the palm of one hand. "I put them together in this apartment so their relationship could progress from where it had gotten to while Josie was staying at Max's ranch."

"That progression may very well have happened," Jeff said, then drained his coffee cup.

"Not that I can tell. I've had regular reports from Gertie. She informed me that there's something between Josie and Max, no doubt about it. She could see it, sense it, even feel it in the air at times. But she said they seemed to be holding back, protecting themselves or some such nonsensical thing.''

"That sounds like Max. Would you like some coffee, Mr. Wentworth?''

"Yes, thank you. Have another cup yourself and drink it slowly. We'll give those two more time to quit acting so foolishly.''

Jeff got to his feet and crossed the large kitchen to get the coffee. He returned with a cup of the steaming liquid for Joseph, then refilled his own cup. When he sat down again at the table, he had a thoughtful expression on his face.

"You know, Mr. Wentworth, I can concoct a story about why we're not going to put a walking cast on Max, after all. He's eligible for one, but I can pretend to have talked to the specialist who has now had second thoughts about it. That would leave Max here in Josie's apartment, stuck in the wheelchair.''

"No,'' Joseph said, shaking his head. "I'm not satisfied with how things went here. More of the same isn't the answer. We'll stall over this coffee. If the ridiculous status quo remains, we'll take Max out the door. Maybe they'll come to their senses if they're not together.''

"This matchmaking stuff is hard work,'' Jeff said.

"It wouldn't be if we were dealing with reasonable people who would follow the program I mapped out.''

"Oh, I see.'' Jeff laughed. "Well, Max Carter, for one, marches to his own drummer.''

"So does Josie Wentworth. The stubborn little minx.''

"I have to say, sir, that I'm more than a bit surprised that you're in favor of a relationship between Josie and Max."

"Why?"

"Well, Max is a good man. He's honest, works hard, and I'm proud to call him my friend. But Max surely wouldn't be able to provide for Josie in the manner she's accustomed to. Max has a fine spread and top-rated cattle, but he's land-poor and doesn't have much money in his pocket."

"I'm aware of all of that," Joseph said. "I had him investigated."

"Oh, Lord, you're kidding." Jeff grinned and shook his head. "Don't ever tell *him* that. He has a major thing about personal privacy. Max would go ballistic if he knew you had someone checking on his background and his day-to-day life."

"I don't intend to tell him. I'm cagey, not stupid. And as for his financial and social status, that doesn't come into consideration when dealing with matters of the heart."

Joseph stared into space for a long moment, then looked at Jeff again.

"My wife, rest her soul, was a waitress in a coffee shop when I met her. My family was already wealthy from Wentworth Oil Works. They gave me nothing but grief about wanting to marry my Emily. She wasn't of 'our class of people,' you see.

"But I married her, anyway, and we had many happy years before she died of heart disease. Josie and Max will have to work out the subject of her money and his lack of it as they see fit." Joseph paused. "If they ever get that far. Mules. That's what they are—stubborn as two mules."

"Yes, sir," Jeff said, chuckling. "I'd say that just about sums it up."

Gertie came into the kitchen. "I'm leaving now, Mr. Wentworth," she said. "I've said my goodbyes to Max and Ms. Wentworth. Max is ready to go, although he didn't eat his breakfast."

"Where's Josie?" Joseph asked.

"She's sitting in a chair in the living room. Both she and Max remind me of pouting children. No disrespect meant, of course."

"I've called them worse than that in the last few minutes," Joseph said. "Thank you for everything, Gertie. You'll be receiving a bonus check in the mail."

"Thank you, sir. This has been a very pleasant and interesting assignment. I must say, however, that if any of my grandchildren ask me to play Candy Land, I'm going to plead a headache. I've had enough of that game to last me the rest of my life. Well, goodbye, and I hope the love bug does a proper job with Ms. Wentworth and Max."

"Goodbye, Gertie," Joseph said.

When the nurse had left the room, Joseph sighed.

"I'm afraid it's going to take more than a bug to set this situation to rights. Do you have any brilliant ideas, Jeff?"

"No, sir, I'm afraid I don't. I believe it's out of our hands now."

"Being in love can be the most wonderful and the

most confusing thing in the world.''

"Yes, sir,'' Jeff said.

Being in love was the pits, Josie thought, slouching lower in the living room chair. She was a befuddled mess, not knowing what to do or say next.

She wanted to leap to her feet, race down the hall and into Max's bedroom. She'd fling herself into his arms, kiss his delicious lips, then tell him she loved him with every breath in her body.

Then euphoric Max, her mind raced on, would smile because of her announcement and declare that he loved her, too, and would until death parted them.

Then she'd tell him about the baby and he'd be thrilled, struck speechless with excitement. They'd return to the Single C and live happily ever after. The end.

"Oh, ha,'' Josie muttered. "Catch the name of that ranch? The *Single* C.''

No, she wasn't going to dash into Max's room with the hope of making her fantasy a reality. She was keeping her bottom planted firmly right here in this chair.

Any second now Jeff and her granddad would appear and whisk Max away.

Any second now.

Tick...tick...tick.

Chapter Fourteen

Josie pressed the damp washcloth more firmly to her forehead and closed her eyes. She lay stretched out on her bed, the curtains drawn across the windows to darken the room.

She had cried—no, she'd wailed very loudly—for nearly two hours after Max had been taken out the door of the apartment.

And what did she have to show for her display of unhappy emotions? A killer of a sinus headache. She also had a heart that felt as though it had splintered into a million pieces, and the same huge, empty, lonely home that had screamed its silence at her before she'd given way to her tears.

"Oh-h-h," Josie moaned. "I'm dying. I won't live through the next hour, and it's all your fault, Max Carter."

There, she thought wryly. How was that statement for exhibiting maturity? Her misery wasn't Max Carter-induced. He hadn't put a gun to her head and ordered her to fall in love with him even though he didn't love her.

No, she had to take responsibility for her own actions. She had failed to be sophisticated enough to have an affair, then walk away, her heart, soul and mind no worse for wear, when it was over.

She hadn't followed the rules. She'd messed up royally by falling deeply and irrevocably in love.

"Dumb, dumb, dumb," Josie said. "Oh-h-h, my poor, aching head."

She sighed and attempted to blank her mind.

If she could sleep, despite it being early afternoon, the slumber might ease the pain in her head. A nap would also give her a reprieve from her despair.

But the oblivion of sleep was elusive. Instead, her mind replayed the final minutes she'd spent with Max over and over.

Jeff had come into the living room and announced that he was going to telephone the ambulance driver, who was waiting down on the street, and would Josie please inform Max that they'd be ready to roll as soon as the men arrived at the apartment with the stretcher?

"Yes, certainly," Josie had said, getting to her feet. "No problem."

No problem? she'd thought, as she'd walked slowly toward Max's bedroom. What a joke.

How could she say goodbye to the man she loved?

How could she say goodbye to the father of the baby she was carrying?

How could she say goodbye, knowing she was facing a future without Max Carter?

Josie had stopped just out of view by the open doorway of Max's room and drew a shaky breath, struggling to control her threatening tears.

She'd counted to ten, then entered the room, making a beeline for the chair next to the bed when she felt her legs begin to tremble. She sat down with a thud and tried to produce a smile, failing miserably.

"Max—" she clasped her hands tightly together in her lap "—Jeff is phoning down to the ambulance now. The attendants will be up to get you in a few minutes."

"Mmm," Max said, frowning.

"I know you'll be so happy to get home to the ranch to make certain everything is all right there. I imagine Rusty will be glad to see you. And your horse. Goodness, your horse must have been wondering where you are. Do horses miss people? Well, sure they do, just like a cat or dog would. Right. Yes, sir, I bet your horse—"

"Josie," Max interrupted.

"Yes?"

"Shut up."

She nodded. "Yes. Good idea. I'm babbling."

"A hundred miles an hour."

"I...I'll miss you, Max," she said. *I love you, Max.* "Very much."

"I'll miss you, too, Josie," he said. *Ah, damn it, Josie Wentworth, I love you.* "Very much."

The baby, Josie thought frantically. She had to tell Max about the baby. He had a right to know. *Just do it, Josie, say it. Tell Max that you're carrying his child.*

"Max, there's something I need to—" she started.

"Down this hallway," they heard Jeff say. "Your patient is ready to go, gentlemen."

"No," Josie whispered.

"Come here." Max extended his arms toward her.

Josie slid onto the edge of the bed and Max wrapped his arms tightly around her. Their lips, their tongues, met in a searing, urgent kiss of want, need and sorrow.

They pressed harder against each other, each feeling so united and complete, yet at the same time so different.

A sob echoed in Josie's ears.

An achy sensation gripped Max's throat.

"Oops and uh-oh," Jeff said cheerfully.

He came into the room, followed by two men propelling a wheeled stretcher. Josie jerked upward, nearly falling off the bed.

"Are you two about finished with the goodbye stuff?" Jeff said. "These fellas and I can just stand here quietly if you need more time."

"Cripes, Wilson," Max said, glowering at him. "You've got as much tact as a rock."

Jeff's eyes widened, and an expression of pure innocence formed on his face.

"What did I do wrong?" he said. "I think I'm being very accommodating here."

"I'll get out of your way," Josie said, starting to rise.

Max grabbed one of her hands. "Josie—"

"Goodbye, Max," she said, her eyes filling with tears. "I wish you every happiness on the Single C. The Single..." Two tears spilled onto her cheeks. "Goodbye, Max Carter."

She'd pulled her hand free and hurried from the room, mumbling, "Excuse me," as she'd made her way around Jeff and the ambulance attendants....

Fresh pain prompted Josie to turn the washcloth over and smack it back onto her forehead.

She'd hidden in her room like a child until Max had gone, finally hollering a farewell to her grandfather through the closed bedroom door.

Then she'd opened the door a crack and peered out, finally moving tentatively into the hallway. She'd stopped in the doorway of the room that had been Max's, and fresh tears had brimmed in her eyes as she stared at the empty bed.

The apartment had been chillingly silent. So empty. Even Max's wheelchair was gone. There were tracks in the plush, white carpeting where the stretcher carrying Max had traveled from his bedroom to the front door.

She'd stood in the quiet living room, unable to tear her gaze from the grooves in the carpeting. When the woman from the cleaning service vacuumed the carpet, the last trace, the final evidence that Max had even been here, would be erased forever....

Josie lowered the washcloth and flattened her hands on her stomach.

There would be no clues left that Max had resided in her home, she thought. But nestled deeply beneath her palms was proof positive that Max Carter had been a very important part of her life for a magical, fairy-tale length of time.

Tick…tick…tick.

And now it was over.

Max was gone.

"Oh, precious baby," Josie whispered in the darkened room. "You have the most magnificent father. I'll tell him about you later when I'm emotionally stronger. Okay?

"But the future is going to be made up of just you and me, little one, together, a team of two. We'll be just fine. Somehow."

Then the tears started again, and Josie wept.

Late that evening Max lay stretched out on his sofa, his head on a pillow, his injured leg propped on another that was balanced on the arm of the faded piece of furniture. He was staring at, but not really seeing, an old Cary Grant movie on television.

He took a deep breath and let it out slowly.

He was bone-weary, too exhausted to move, and the pain in his leg had increased from the level of one toothache to about five.

Jeff had assured him that he'd feel much better tomorrow. Changing a cast definitely caused discomfort, he'd said, but it would quiet down quickly. He'd given Max a metal cane to keep from putting his entire weight on the leg when he walked.

All in all, Max mused, the broken-leg situation

was much improved. Being able to walk around was great. Hell, he'd even managed to get on a pair of jeans by slitting the seam of the soft, worn material partway up one side of the right leg.

He would feel better tomorrow, he mentally repeated. Yes, he would.

At least physically he'd be up and at it.

The ranch had obviously been extremely well tended by Rusty, Max's own hands and the men Joseph Wentworth had hired. He'd have Rusty take him on a full tour of the spread in the morning, but the little he'd seen indicated that everything was shipshape.

Joseph had firmly declared that the extra men were to remain on the ranch until Max's leg was totally healed and he was operating at full capacity. So be it. He didn't have the energy to argue with the mighty, my-directives-are-always-followed Mr. Wentworth.

He would feel better tomorrow.

"Yeah, right," Max said aloud.

When Jeff had promised that, the good doctor hadn't known he should add a very important factor to the equation—his buddy, Max Carter, had walked—well, been wheeled—away from the woman he loved.

Max Carter had said goodbye to Josie.

He could see Josie so clearly in his mind's eye, see the tears on her pale cheeks as they'd said those last farewells. He'd wanted to grab hold of her, wrap his arms around her so tightly, refuse to let her go and bring her home with him—forever.

He'd wanted to declare his love for her, then ask her straight out if she was in love with him.

He'd wanted to babble the way Josie did at times, spill out plans for a future together—marriage, babies, the wondrous sound of joyous laughter singing through the air on the Single C.

But he'd done nothing more than quietly say goodbye to her.

He had nothing to offer except his love, and that wouldn't be enough, not for a Wentworth.

His shabby little house was a world and a heartbreak away from a penthouse apartment with plush, white carpeting.

"I love you, Josie," Max said aloud. "You'll never know that, but I love you so much."

He sighed, then closed his eyes, welcoming the somnolence that began to creep over him, welcoming the escape from the stark, cold reality of his loneliness.

At dawn on the third day after Max had left her apartment and her life, Josie made her routine dash to the bathroom, where she repeated over and over in her mind that she would survive this bout of morning sickness as she had the previous ones.

When she crept back into bed on trembling legs, she waited for the tears to begin. But they didn't come. Instead, she narrowed her eyes and stared up at the ceiling.

Enough of this weeping and wailing, she told herself. *She was a Wentworth.* She didn't quit when the going got rough. She didn't give up, curl into a ball of misery and refuse to face the challenge before her. She lifted her chin, squared her shoulders and fought for what she was determined to have.

Josie stilled as a whispering little voice in her head nudged for attention, gaining volume as she strained to hear it.

Jack be nimble. Jack be quick. Jack...

"Oh, God, Jack," she said, blinking away sudden tears. "I hear you, Jack. You're telling me to be brave and strong just as you did all those years ago.

"I love Max Carter very much. I'm going to fight for him. I am. Did you love Sabrina Jensen, Jack? Did you find love, just as I have, before you died? I hope so. Oh, my darling brother, I hope you did."

Jack be nimble. Jack be quick.

"Carter," Josie said, leaving the bed, "the war is on. Gear up for battle, cowboy, because I'm coming after you. The only thing that can defeat me will be if you don't love me the way I love you."

She showered and washed her hair, then forced herself to eat a nutritious breakfast. She entered her library, settled onto the soft leather chair behind the desk, then picked up the telephone receiver.

After speaking with the information operator, she punched in the numbers she'd been given. The other end of the line was picked up on the third ring.

"Hello?"

"Sally? This is Josie Wentworth."

"Oh, Josie, how marvelous to hear your voice," Sally said. "I've been pestering Jeff to death with questions about how you're doing. I miss having you in our part of the country."

"I miss you, too, Sally, and—" Josie lifted her chin "—I miss that stubborn Max Carter more than I can even begin to tell you."

"Wonderful. Super. Jeff was over at the Single C yesterday and he said that Max isn't fit to live with. He's grumpy, short-tempered, barking orders at everyone like a drill sergeant.

"If your grandfather wasn't paying those extra hands so well to work there, they'd be long gone. Max's own guys are threatening to quit, and Rusty is just hiding out in the barn."

"Interesting," Josie murmured. "Very interesting."

"Max would probably bite his own tongue off before he'd say it," Sally went on, "but I truly believe that the way he's acting is because he misses you terribly, Josie. He may even be...well..."

"In love with me?"

"All the signs are there, that's for sure, but Max isn't your run-of-the-mill man."

"I know," Josie said, smiling. "Oh, yes, that fact is a magnificent given." She paused. "Sally, I love Max Carter with every fiber of my body."

"You do?" Sally said, with an excited squeak. "You really do?"

"I really do," Josie said decisively.

"Oh, I'm going to cry. This is so romantic, so—"

"Sally," Josie interrupted, "it isn't going to be one bit romantic if Max isn't in love with *me*."

"Yes, well, you've got a point there."

"So, Max's true feelings for me have to be determined. Then there's the problem of Max's pride. You know, my being a Wentworth, my money, my social status."

"This is getting depressing," Sally said. "Your being a Wentworth is no small matter."

"I realize that. Sally, I need your help—yours and Jeff's."

"You've got it. Do you have a plan?"

"Oh, yes." Josie laughed. "I most definitely have a plan."

"What is it? Tell me. Tell me."

"It would be better to speak with you and Jeff at the same time. I'll telephone you this evening and you two can be on separate extensions. All right?"

"I'll go nuts waiting that long. Jeff said he'd be home for lunch today. Couldn't the three of us talk then?"

"No, I won't be here. I have to go to the public library."

"The public library? What on earth for?"

"I've got a great deal of studying to do on the subject of ranch management."

"What?"

"I'll talk to you tonight."

"Okay. We'll be eager for the phone to ring. Bye for now."

"Goodbye, Sally, and thank you so much."

Josie replaced the receiver, planted her hands on the desk and pushed herself to her feet. Before leaving her library she recited in her mind once more the words from her source of courage.

Jack be nimble. Jack be quick.

Chapter Fifteen

Early the next afternoon, Max sat on the top front-porch step of his house, scowling at nothing in particular.

During one of the telephone conversations he'd had with Rusty while he'd been staying at Josie's, Max had instructed the older man to have one of the hands repair the sagging front steps. Also, Max had instructed his friend to grab some white paint from the sheds and have one of the hands slap some on the entire porch. He turned his head to study the results of his directives.

Not bad, he thought. It was amazing what a little paint could do to improve the appearance of something. It wouldn't hurt to roll some paint on the walls inside the house, too.

Max's gaze shifted to the perfectly manicured little

patch of grass in his front yard. His glowering expression returned full force.

It was getting pretty bad, he thought, when a plot of green grass caused a knot to tighten in his gut and visions of Josie to slam front-row center in his mind's eye.

She'd put in so many hours shaping up that yard, Max thought. She'd trimmed her fancy nails, then sunk those lovely hands into the dirt, obviously enjoying every minute of her self-assigned project.

He could remember how amazed he'd been that a Wentworth would willingly get covered in mud while crawling on hands and knees to pull weeds. Even though Josie hadn't known who she really was at the time, he'd expected her lifetime of being pampered to be ingrained.

But now that he knew Josie so well, loved Josie so much, her determination to spruce up that crummy yard didn't surprise him in the least. There were a multitude of fascinating, wonderful facets to Josie.

She was like a precious gift wrapped in endless layers of gorgeous paper, waiting to be carefully, reverently brushed aside, one by one.

Cripes, Carter, listen to yourself. Talk about corny. Where was all this stuff coming from? He didn't sit around thinking like this.

You just did, a voice in his head taunted.

He did a lot of things differently since Josie Wentworth had entered his life and captured his heart.

He smiled more, and felt the freeing joy of laughing right out loud whenever the mood struck.

Josie had taught him that.

He'd adapted a better balance to his workday,

leaving time and energy for relaxing, pleasant evenings.

Josie had taught him that.

He'd come to understand the difference between personal privacy and sharing.

Josie had taught him that.

If they'd had more time together, he probably would have kicked aside the few remaining bricks in the wall he'd built around himself. He'd have told her about his youth, his respect for his hardworking father, the pain his mother's desertion had caused both father and son, his own fears about loving someone because of what had happened to him as a boy.

But he and Josie had run out of time.

Everything they'd had together was over.

And he'd never be the same again.

"Ah, hell," Max said, yanking his Stetson low on his forehead. "Quit thinking, Carter." He looked in the direction of the road leading to the house. "Come on, Wilson. You said it was important that you see me, so get your butt over here."

As though having heard Max's grumpy command, a cloud of dust appeared in the distance, then Jeff's car came into view.

"It's about time," Max muttered.

He grabbed his cane, maneuvered himself upward, then started slowly forward on the narrow, cracked, weed-free sidewalk. He squinted his eyes as the car drew closer, the angle of the sun causing a bright glare, making it impossible to see inside the vehicle.

Jeff stopped the car, got out and closed the door.

"Howdy, buddy," Jeff said, smiling. "How are you?"

"Bored," Max said, not returning Jeff's smile.

"You've arrived twenty minutes later than you said you would. I've got work to do, so what's on your mind?"

"You'll never win the congeniality contest, Carter," Jeff said cheerfully. "Your mood these days is worse than a bear with a thorn in its paw."

"How folksy. Cut to the chase, Wilson. What's so all-fired important that you had to pull me off the range to discuss it with you?"

"Okay, okay," Jeff said, raising both hands. "There's a problem. Big time. And I need your help."

"What kind of a problem?"

"Josie."

Max stiffened, every muscle in his body tensing, causing a hot pain to shoot through his injured leg.

"Josie?" he said. "What's wrong with her? Has something happened to her? Damn it, Jeff, tell me."

"Stay calm," Jeff said. "I'll explain everything in a minute."

Jeff moved around to the passenger side of the car and opened the door. A moment later Max's eyes widened and his heart began to thunder.

Josie was here? he thought incredulously. Yes, there she was, only twenty feet away. She was coming toward him, wearing a pretty rose-colored dress and a white gauze bandage on one side of her forehead.

A bandage? On her head? Josie was hurt?

Max started to move, only to have the tip of the cane catch in a crack in the sidewalk and halt his step.

Josie stopped in front of him, a pleasant little smile on her face. Jeff stood directly behind her.

"Hello," Josie said, extending her hand toward Max. "I'm Josie Wentworth. And you are?"

Max stared at Josie's hand, her face, her hand, then looked at her again.

"Huh?" he said.

"Darn it," Jeff said, snapping his fingers. "We were hoping that seeing you would solve this immediately." He sighed, very deeply and very dramatically. "Well, so be it. It's just going to be more complicated than that."

"What in the hell is going on here?" Max roared.

"My goodness, sir," Josie said. "It's isn't necessary to yell." She touched one fingertip gingerly to the bandage. "Your hollering is making my headache worse, thank you very much." She paused. "Who did you say you were? Oh, that's right, you didn't say. So, who are you?"

"That cooks it," Max said. "Wilson, in the house. Now. I've got questions and I want answers."

Max turned and, as much as his injured leg would allow, stomped up the sidewalk, across the porch and into the house, leaving the door open behind him.

"So far, so good," Josie said as she and Jeff started after Max. "I'll be in the house, which is exactly where I need to be."

"Max is a tad hot under the collar," Jeff said, shaking his head.

True, Josie thought. But her Max was also magnificently, ruggedly handsome. It had taken all the willpower she possessed to keep from flinging herself into his arms, peppering his wonderful face with kisses, then shouting at the top of her lungs that she loved him.

"All set?" Jeff whispered as they approached the open doorway.

"Yes," Josie whispered back.

"You're doing great so far. You almost had *me* convinced you don't know who Max is."

"I've got to pull this off, Jeff. I need time alone with Max. I've got to make him listen. Our happiness—our entire future together—is at stake." She paused. "I hope Sally's call comes at the right time."

"She's standing by to do her part. I think we're right on schedule."

"Wilson!" Max bellowed from inside the house.

"Man, oh, man," Jeff said. "I feel as though I'm throwing you into the lion's den, then hightailing it to safety. Are you sure you should—"

"Positive," Josie said. "Onward and upward, partner-in-crime."

They entered the house and saw Max sprawled in a chair in the living room, his arms crossed firmly on his chest. His Stetson was teetering on the edge of the coffee table, where he'd obviously tossed it.

"Sit," Max said. "Speak."

"Josie—" Jeff turned to her as she settled onto the sofa "—this is Max Carter. He owns this ranch."

"The Single C." She folded her hands primly in her lap. "Yes, I saw the name in the metal scrollwork when we turned onto the road leading to the house. It's a pleasure to make your acquaintance, Mr. Carter. Max. May I call you Max?"

"Wilson..." Max said, his jaw tight and a warning in his voice.

"Right." Jeff cleared his throat as he remained standing halfway between the sofa and chair. "Here's the scoop, Max. Josie took a spill in her apartment. Her grandfather was taking her out to dinner and Josie was wearing high-heeled shoes. One of them caught in the carpeting and she tumbled forward, striking her forehead on the edge of an end table.''

''I always said that carpeting was ridiculous.'' Max's voice was gruff. ''Thick, white carpeting in a home? Cripes.''

''It's not entirely white anymore,'' Josie said. ''My poor little head bled all over it.''

''You were bleeding?'' Max straightened in his chair. ''How much blood did you lose? How badly are you hurt?''

''I have the floor, Max,'' Jeff said. ''Just shut up and listen.''

Max slouched back in the chair and glared at Jeff.

''Anyway,'' Jeff continued, ''the cut on Josie's head isn't all that bad. It only took a few stitches to close it, and she shouldn't have much of a scar. The thing is, she lost part of her memory again.''

''Which is so annoying,'' Josie said with a sigh.

''I've consulted extensively with the experts that Joseph Wentworth brought in,'' Jeff went on. ''Josie's condition isn't common, but it's not unheard of, either. This bump, following so closely behind her concussion, has reactivated her amnesia—to a lesser degree than before, though. She's just missing some slices of time.

''The experts agreed it might be beneficial to bring Josie here, because her stay at the Single C is one of the missing slices.''

''You don't remember even being here, Josie?'' Max said incredulously. ''With me?''

''Nope,'' Josie said pleasantly. ''I don't even remember *you.* I've been told you were a guest in my home after I was a guest here in yours. But—" she shrugged "—poof. All memories of those visits are gone."

Josie didn't remember that they'd made love? Max thought. He didn't like this, not one damn bit. He'd been erased from her life, like a smudge on a piece of paper.

No way. He wasn't taking this sitting down. He couldn't have a future with her, but by damn, Josie was going to remember what they'd shared in the past.

"So you brought Josie here to jog her memory?" Max said to Jeff. "But it didn't work."

"No, it sure didn't," Jeff said, frowning. "So, on to plan B. Josie is—"

A beeping noise cut through the air.

"My pager," Jeff said much too loudly. "I must use the telephone, Max. I'll go into the kitchen to do that. Goodbye."

As an actor, Josie thought, Jeff Wilson was a dismal flop. Oh, well.

"So, tell me, Max," Josie said when Jeff disappeared from view. "Were we spending time in each other's homes to discuss a business venture? I wasn't told anything other than that I came here to see you, injured my head and stayed on. You later came to my home. Were we working out the details of our business partnership?"

"Business partnership?" Max said. "What kind of business would we be in together?"

"I'm launching my own little company. I'm in ranch management. You know, putting all a rancher's records on computer, including the status of the cattle, the whole nine yards. Were you to be my first client?"

Max leaned slightly forward. "You're really going to take that on as a career?"

"Oh, my, yes. I've been studying my heart out. I love it. It's very challenging. I know how many acres are needed for each head of cattle to be properly nourished, when various breeds are best taken to market, how to—"

"Cut," Max said, slicing one hand through the air. "Just how did you propose to manage my ranch without living here on the spread?"

Josie frowned and pressed one fingertip to her chin. "I can't remember." She brightened. "Do you know how we planned to accomplish that?"

By getting married! Max's mind thundered. By pledging our love with sacred vows, by becoming husband and wife. *Ah, Carter, can it.* He was daydreaming again.

"No," he said quietly. "I have no idea how that could come about."

We'd get married! Josie thought frantically. We'd live and love and laugh right here on this ranch and raise our miracle, our child.

"Oh," she said.

"Josie, I didn't even know you were starting a business of ranch management. I think it's great, I really do, but that's not why we were together."

Jeff came whizzing back into the room.

"I have to hustle," he said. "I have a mother-to-be in labor with twins."

"Who?" Max said.

"Who?" Jeff echoed. "Oh, um, Mary-Amber

Henderson. Josie, I'll leave your suitcase on the porch."

"What suitcase?" Max said.

"The experts said that if coming here didn't set things to rights straight off, Josie should stay on for a spell," Jeff declared. "I've got to run. Twins have a tendency to be in a hurry to be born. I'll check in with you later. Bye."

"Ta-ta," Josie said, waggling the fingers of one hand in the air. She paused, waiting for the sound of the front door closing. "I want to thank you for your cooperation in letting me stay here, Max. I'll try not to be a nuisance."

Mmm," Max said.

"Jeff mentioned that you aren't married, but that doesn't mean there isn't a special woman in your life. I hope my being here won't cause any difficulties between you and that someone special."

"Don't worry about it." Max's frown deepened. "There was someone special, but it...it didn't work out."

Josie's heart did a funny little two-step, and she had to struggle to keep the pleasant expression on her face.

"Oh?" she said. "I'm sorry. Would you like to talk about it? Sometimes it helps to share with someone, to get it out in the open where you can deal with it better.

"You know me, but I really don't know you. It would be like unburdening yourself to a stranger, which might make it easier. I'd be more than willing to listen."

Max ran one hand over his chin and stared at Josie. Pour out his pain, his heartache about losing Josie to

Josie Wentworth herself? That would be the dumbest thing he'd ever done.

But then again…

He'd spent his life bottling everything up inside, handling it all in solitude. But since he'd met Josie he'd lost most of his protective wall, had come to look forward to talking with her. He'd learned the difference between personal privacy and sharing—and sharing won, hands down.

As crazy as it was, maybe he could be free of the crushing weight of loneliness, the icy chill caused by missing Josie, by looking right at her while he explained why their worlds could never mesh.

It was worth a try. Hell, he couldn't go on the way he was. With Josie being in the midst of another bout of amnesia, she'd never have a clue that he was talking about them.

Hell, why not? Anything was better than the emotional agony he'd been through since leaving her. When she regained her memory and realized he'd been speaking about them, she'd know he'd dealt with his loss and why he was moving forward with his life, alone.

"You wouldn't mind hearing my woes?" he said.

"Not at all." Josie wriggled farther back on the sofa. "There. I'm all settled in. You go right ahead and share, Max, and I'll listen."

Please, Max, she silently begged. *This is our last chance.* She'd concocted this desperate plan with the hope, prayer, that stubborn, prideful Max Carter would bare his soul, step from behind the last remaining bricks of his protective wall, so she could reach out to him, fully, at long last. *Please, please,*

Max. Do it. For us. For our baby. I love you so much.

Max gripped the arms of the chair, not realizing his hold was so tight his knuckles were turning white.

"Yeah, well, there is...was a woman," he said, "who came into my life and I... But she..." He shook his head. "No, I can't do this."

"Yes, you can. You must." Josie strove to keep her voice from trembling. "The woman came into your life and...?"

"Okay, okay. She's very wealthy, comes from a prominent family." He swept his eyes over the small room, then met Josie's gaze again. "Look at this place. It's shabby. I'm a land-poor rancher, nothing more, and it's not enough."

"Did she say that?" Josie said, her heart beating so wildly she could hear it in her ears.

"Well, no, not really. *I* said it, to myself. We pretended for a while that it didn't matter, created a fantasy world built on stolen time."

"That sounds wonderful," Josie said softly.

"It was, it truly was. She changed me, taught me so much about sharing and caring. But the truth couldn't be ignored forever. So now? It's over. I'm in my world. She's in hers. The end."

This was it, Josie thought, fighting against threatening tears. She was about to ask the question that would determine all the tomorrows yet to come.

"Max?" she said, her voice hardly above a whisper. "Are you in love with her? Do you love her with all your heart?"

A muscle jumped in Max's jaw. He stared up at the ceiling for a long moment, took a deep breath, then let it out slowly. When he looked at Josie again, a sob caught in her throat as she saw the raw pain radiating from the dark depths of Max's eyes.

"Yes," he said, his voice raspy with emotion. "Yes, I'm in love with her. I want her to be my wife, the mother of my children, my life partner. She'll never know that, though, because I have nothing to offer her."

Oh, dear God, Josie thought, Max loved her, just as she loved him. She wanted to run across the room, fling herself into his arms and never let him go. But no, she had to control her soaring emotions. Everything hung in the balance now, depended on her saying exactly the right words to this magnificent man.

She pressed one hand onto her stomach, envisioning her and Max's child nestled there.

Courage, Josie, she told herself. Reach deeply for courage and womanly wisdom.

Jack be nimble. Jack be quick.

Josie lifted her chin and looked directly into Max's eyes.

"Is she in love with you, Max?"

"I don't know. She cares for me deeply. She wouldn't take what we shared together lightly. I think...yes, maybe, she might be in love with me. But, hell, she knows as well as I do that we can't have a future together. What would have been the point in telling me that she loves me? I didn't tell *her* how I really felt, either."

"Let's assume she's in love with you."

"Whatever." Max released his tight hold on the chair and crossed his arms over his chest again. "This conversation is getting ridiculous."

"No, it's not. It's important," Josie said, a slightly

frantic edge to her voice. "There's a solution to the problem of your opposite worlds."

"Yeah, right. Wave a magic wand and make her as poor as a church mouse."

"Max, please, listen to me. Please?"

He shrugged. "Go for it."

"You each bring things from your worlds and mesh them into one entity. She's wealthy? Fine. Let her build a big, rambling, sunny house here on the ranch were your children can grow up. Your love will fill that house, turn it into a home ringing with laughter and joy."

"Pretty picture," Max said sarcastically. "What in the hell am *I* adding to the pot?"

Josie leaned forward, wrapping her arms around her stomach.

"Oh, Max, don't you see? You would bring, along with your love, the wonder of the land, of fresh air and sunshine, and freedom to run through fields of wildflowers. You'd teach your children the lessons of working hard and reaping the rewards of that work."

Tears spilled onto Josie's cheeks and she dashed them away.

"And, Max?" she said, tears echoing in her voice. "When the leaves turn color in the fall, you'd all go walking in the woods as the wind whispered through the trees and you'd hear the song of autumn.

"You have nothing to offer her? Oh, Max, you have precious gifts to give her and your children, along with your love."

Max pushed himself to his feet, teetering for a moment on his cast-covered leg.

"That's what my father thought a lifetime ago.

But guess what? My mother didn't want any of it. She left. She just packed up and took off."

There they went, Josie thought, the last bricks of Max's wall had just fallen. *Oh, my darling, my beloved Max.*

"Stop for a second and think," she said softly. "Think about the woman you love. Don't make her pay the price for what your mother did. If your lady really loves you, Max, would she ever leave you if you allowed her to stay by your side? Look deep into your heart. Would she leave you?"

Max drew a shuddering breath. "No. No, not my Josie. Once she makes up her mind about something...no..."

"No, I would never leave you," Josie said, rising to her feet. "Because I love you, Max Carter. I love you with all that I am, and you love me. Oh, Max, please, let me come home."

Max narrowed his eyes. "Take that bandage off your head."

Josie tore off the gauze, lifted her chin and squared her shoulders.

"There's nothing wrong with your head," Max said, none too quietly. "This was a game, a sham."

"A hope and a prayer," Josie said. "We *can* mesh our worlds, Max, if you let us. We can have it all."

"You really love me?"

"With all my heart."

"You'd build a house and I'd—"

"Give us the song of autumn."

"Oh, God, Josie," Max said, his voice choked with emotion. He opened his arms to her. "Come here."

And Josie went.

She flung herself into Max's embrace, nearly toppling them over. Their lips met in a kiss that was a commitment to forever and caused their loneliness and pain to be chased into oblivion, never to return.

The kiss was love.

Much later they lay close together on Max's bed, sated from lovemaking, at peace.

Max splayed one hand on Josie's flat stomach.

"Unbelievable," he said. "A baby. Our child. Ah, Josie, you've given me so much, brought such happiness into my empty life. Will you marry me?"

"What I've given you matches what you've given me, Max. And, yes, I'll marry you." She paused. "We'll have Jeff deliver our baby."

"Yep." Max frowned, then burst into laughter.

"What's so funny?"

"It just registered in my thick head. Jeff was so shook up trying to pull off his part in your fabulous plan that he really messed up. He said Mary-Amber Henderson was in labor with twins."

"Yes. So?"

"Mary-Amber Henderson is seventy-two years old."

Their mingled laughter danced through the air, creating a new and wondrous song that would be theirs forever.

Epilogue

Josie stood in front of the calendar on the wall of Max's kitchen, staring at the squares of numbers.

"Mail call," Max yelled, coming in the front door. He entered the kitchen. "What's so interesting about the calendar?"

"I just realized that Thanksgiving will be here before we know it," Josie said, smiling at him. "I wonder if I can learn how to cook a turkey by then?"

"Sweetheart, I don't think so." Max chuckled as he sifted through the stack of mail. "Why don't we accept your grandfather's very generous offer to fly us to Freemont Springs in the company plane and share the holiday with him and your brother, Michael? We'll eat turkey prepared by your Evvie."

"That sounds perfect."

"Hey, here's the application form I requested to change the brand for the ranch," Max said, looking at an envelope. "We'll fill this out, mail it in, and we'll soon be the Double C."

"What about the baby?"

Max dropped a quick kiss on her lips. "Josie, I want a slew of kids, but the rumps on cattle are just so big, you know. Let's settle for a brand that represents only you and me, because we'll still be here together when those children are grown and off finding their places in the world."

"You're a wise man, Max Carter," Josie said, wrapping her arms around his waist.

"Hey, look at this." He handed an envelope to Josie. "It's addressed to Sabrina. Go ahead and open it."

Josie took the piece of mail. "Max, are you certain you're comfortable about opening Sabrina's personal mail?"

"Yes. I don't know where my cousin is, and maybe this will give us a clue. If your brother, Jack, really did love Sabrina and she loved him, then she's lonely and in pain. She needs her family, just as your grandfather needs to connect with her, if she was to become Jack's wife."

"Thank you, Max," Josie said, love shining in her big, dark eyes.

"You've taught me a great many important things, Josie. Open the envelope."

Josie did as instructed, and Max read the enclosed piece of paper over her shoulder.

"It's a bill," he said. "From Dr. Amanda Lucas in Mason's Grove. That's a small town between Tulsa and Stillwater."

"Dr. Lucas is an OB/GYN," Josie said. "Oh, how frustrating. We have no way of knowing if Sabrina saw Amanda Lucas for her obstetrics specialty, or the gynecology. Physician confidentiality will, no doubt, keep Dr. Lucas from telling us.''

''Yep.''

''Wait a minute,'' Josie said. ''I thought the name Mason's Grove sounded familiar. There's an old family friend who lives there. Sam Arquette.

''Max, I'm going to telephone Sam and ask him to, well, sort of check out Amanda Lucas, see if he can discover if there's any chance at all she might be sympathetic to our need to find Sabrina.''

''It's worth a try, my love,'' Max said.

Josie turned and lifted the telephone receiver.

* * * * *

FOLLOW THAT BABY
into Silhouette Romance
in November 1998
when star author Kristin Morgan
tells the emotional, heartwarming story of
THE DADDY AND THE BABY DOCTOR.

And in future months, look for these fabulous titles:

THE SHERIFF AND THE IMPOSTOR BRIDE
by Elizabeth Bevarly,
Desire, December 1998

THE MILLIONAIRE AND THE PREGNANT PAUPER
by Christie Ridgway,
Yours Truly, January 1999

THE MERCENARY AND THE NEW MOM
by Merline Lovelace,
Intimate Moments, February 1999

Turn the page for a
sneak preview of the next fabulous

FOLLOW THAT BABY *title,*

THE DADDY AND THE BABY DOCTOR
by star author Kristin Morgan,

available in Silhouette Romance
in November 1998....

Sam Arquette paused momentarily to study the engraved brass name plate on the office door. It read Amanda Lucas, M.D. Turning the knob, he stepped inside and in one swift glance saw that the waiting room was full.

Full of pregnant women.

Well, he had been halfway expecting as much. Amanda Lucas's reputation as one of the best OB/GYN specialists in Mason's Grove, Oklahoma, was almost godlike. If he had learned anything at all about her in the past few hours, it was that she was considered the town's baby doctor extraordinaire. But the truth of the matter was, he wasn't here to see Amanda Lucas because the good folks in Mason's Grove thought the world of her. He was here as a favor to a friend.

If it hadn't been for the favor Josie Wentworth had

asked of him, he would have been at home right this minute, doing chores around his small farm while enjoying the company of his two young children. It was his way of life these days, although sometimes the fact that it was still surprised him.

In truth, he really didn't mind doing this favor for Josie. He wanted to help the Wentworths all he could. He and Jack Wentworth, Josie's older brother, had been Navy buddies, and the best of friends. Now Jack was dead, killed only recently while on an undercover mission. It seemed impossible that it could be true, but it was. And now the Wentworths were looking for a young woman whom they believed was involved with Jack right before his death. But, according to Josie, the woman had literally disappeared. Luckily, Josie had come across a doctor's statement that suggested the woman might be living in Mason's Grove. And since he now lived in the small Oklahoma town, Josie had asked him to look into the matter for her.

Clearing his throat, Sam pushed aside the sad thought that his good friend Jack was dead and, like the disciplined soldier he was, in spite of his retirement, he focused his full attention on accomplishing his mission.

Answers. He wanted answers. For Josie and her family. For Jack. And for himself, too.

Sam cautiously surveyed the crowded waiting room. From the looks of things he figured he had made a mistake coming to Amanda Lucas's office without calling for an appointment first. But as full-time daddy to his girls, he had to seize opportunities when they arose. His world revolved around his girls. It was as simple as that.

And as complicated.

He had been ill-prepared to assume the responsibility of being a single parent. At the time of his wife's death, he had known more about disarming a nuclear weapon than he had about the nutritional needs of his kids. He had come a long way in the past months. Suzy Homemaker, he was not. But he was getting there.

Still, although he was settling down to a more normal way of life than he had ever dreamed possible for himself, all within a blink of an eye of Josie Wentworth's phone call, he had felt the same old familiar stirrings of excitement that used to accompany him on every SEABEE mission he had ever gone on. Some things, it seemed, never changed. He was about as far away from that world as he could possibly get, and yet, deep down inside, he really wasn't that far away at all. Nor would he ever be, he now realized. Once a soldier, always a soldier.

Not that he was expecting this favor he was doing for the Wentworths to be any kind of a challenge. Good grief, he had just come here to ask the good lady-doctor a few questions about one of her patients. Just how difficult could that be?

Squaring his shoulders, Sam started forward, his eyes fixed on the receptionist area at the rear of the waiting room. It took him five long strides to reach the counter. Meanwhile, he couldn't help but notice that the decor in the room was leaning toward a very feminine influence. In fact, he was beginning to feel like a bull in a China shop.

The receptionist looked up and greeted him with a smile. "Hi. Can I help you?"

He grinned. "I'm Sam Arquette. I'm here to see the doctor."

"I see," she replied hesitantly. Then she cocked her head to one side. "You know, don't you, that Doc Lucas is an OB/GYN physician? All of her patients are women."

"I'm quite aware of that fact," Sam replied. "Look, I'll only take up a moment of her time."

"I'm sorry," the receptionist replied. "But unless you have an emergency, Dr. Lucas won't see you without an appointment."

Already Sam was shaking his head. "You don't understand. My business with Dr. Lucas is extremely important. I must see her now—today." He crossed his arms over his chest. "In fact, I'm not leaving here until I do."

After giving him a thoughtful frown, the young receptionist said, "Okay, if it's that urgent, I'll see what I can do."

Within a couple of minutes, she was back. "This must be your lucky day, Mr. Arquette," she announced. "Doc Lucas has agreed to see you. Follow me. I'll take you to her office."

Moments later, alone in Amanda Lucas's office, Sam sat down to wait for his meeting with her. Minutes passed. Long, endless minutes. Finally, he picked up the only magazine he saw lying around and began reading an article on breast feeding. He figured he might as well learn something while he waited.

"Mr. Arquette, I presume."

The voice was definitely female, but it was deep and sultry and immediately sent tingles down his spine. There was no doubt in his mind that, under just the right circumstances, a voice like that could have easily enthralled a man—in fact, encompass his whole being. But, Sam reminded himself, this wasn't the right circumstance.

Besides, even if it was, he wasn't interested. He already had his hands full, raising his two young daughters.

Shaking himself free of those errant thoughts, Sam sat up straight and then turned in his seat to see a woman with shoulder-length brown hair standing just a few feet inside the doorway. She had a stethoscope around her neck, and she wore a long white lab coat over her street clothes. She had clear blue eyes and a full mouth that, for the moment, at least, lacked the semblance of a smile.

But her voice... It was deep, and throaty and incredibly sexy. Not just any woman deserved to have a voice like that.

Taking a deep, steadying breath, Sam stood and quickly offered her his hand. "And you must be Dr. Lucas," he said evenly. Get a grip, he told himself. He hadn't thought—nor wanted to think—of a woman in quite this way sincc...well, since forever, it seemed. And, frankly, he was shaken to the core.

Amanda Lucas was shaken, too. The tall, muscular man standing before her was extremely good-looking, and for some reason that bothered her. She folded her arms across her chest and peered down at the hand he was offering her. He had strong, capable-looking hands. Still, Amanda was contemplating whether or not to shake hands. So far her impression of Sam Arquette was that he was impulsive and arrogant. Not only that, but she was almost certain he was the same person who had been going around town earlier in the day, asking questions about her. Several of her patients had told her about him. But, finally, she resigned herself to the inevitable and slipped her hand into his, only to discover his palm was surprisingly warm. Ending the handshake as quickly as possible, she straightened her shoulders. "I'm a very busy person, Mr. Arquette. What, may I ask, is so urgent that you had to see me about it today?"

"I need to ask you some questions about one of your patients."

Amanda frowned. "Is that why you were snooping around town today, asking questions about me?"

"You know about that?" Sam asked, an incredulous look spreading across his face.

"Mason's Grove is a small town. News travels fast here."

"I can explain," Sam said, moving a step closer to her.

He looked menacing in a sort of nonthreatening way. If that was possible. She was determined to hold her ground.

"Let me explain something to you, Mr. Arquette," she said, giving him a hard glare. Still, her heart was beating wildly. Too wildly. She dropped her eyes from his as soon as she could. "Any information I have concerning my patients is strictly confidential between them and me."

"I understand how you must feel about that, but—"

"There are no buts," she said, interrupting him. Frankly, she wanted to end this conversation as soon as possible. She needed oxygen and there simply wasn't enough in her office right now for the two of them. "Now, if you'll excuse me, I've got a busy schedule. I'll have my receptionist show you out." With that, she headed straight past him for the door.

"You're making a mistake," Sam said. "This could be a matter of life and death."

A moment passed while Amanda paused in the doorway. Finally, she spun on her heels to face him. "Okay, Mr. Arquette. You've got my undivided attention. But this better be damned good."

COMING NEXT MONTH

#1207 A FAMILY KIND OF GAL—Lisa Jackson
That Special Woman!
Forever Family
All Tiffany Santini wanted was a life of harmony away from her domineering in-laws. But a long-ago attraction was reignited when her sinfully sexy brother in-law, J.D., decided this single mom needn't raise her kids all alone. Could he tempt Tiffany to surrender all her love—to him?

#1208 THE COWGIRL & THE UNEXPECTED WEDDING—Sherryl Woods
And Baby Makes Three: The Next Generation
Once, headstrong Lizzy Adams had captured Hank Robbins's heart, but he'd reluctantly let her go. Now they were together again, and their pent-up passion couldn't be denied. What would it take for a fit-to-be-tied cowboy to convince a mule-headed mother-to-be to march down the aisle?

#1209 PRINCE CHARMING, M.D.—Susan Mallery
Prescription: Marriage
Just about every nurse at Honeygrove Memorial Hospital was swooning shamelessly over debonair doc Trevor MacAllister. All except disillusioned Dana Rowan, who vowed to never, ever wed a doctor—much less be lured by Trevor's Prince Charming act again. But *some* fairy tales are destined to come true....

#1210 UNTIL YOU—Janis Reams Hudson
Timid Anna Collins knew what to expect from her quiet, predictable life. Until she discovered a sexy stranger sleeping on her sofa. Suddenly her uninvited houseguest made it his mission to teach her about all of life's pleasures. Would he stick around for the part about when a man loves a woman?

#1211 A MOTHER FOR JEFFREY—Trisha Alexander
Leslie Marlowe was doing a good job of convincing herself that she wasn't meant to be anyone's wife—or mother. But then young Jeffrey Canfield came into her life, followed by his strong, sensitive father, Brian. Now the only thing Leslie had to convince herself of was that she wasn't dreaming!

#1212 THE RANCHER AND THE REDHEAD—Allison Leigh
Men of the Double-C Ranch
Matthew Clay was set in his ways—and proud of it, too. So when virginal city gal Jaimie Greene turned his well-ordered ranch into Calamity Central, the sassy redhead had him seething with anger and consumed with desire. Dare he open his home—and his heart—to the very *last* woman he should love?